Jake pulled [...] unexpected suddenness.

A bullet whistled past them, followed by another.

"Run for the glacier. I'll cover you." He stood like a human shield and returned fire.

Beth ran, propelled by sheer terror. She stumbled and slipped, righting herself. The ground became silt-covered ice. She'd made it to the glacier. Now what?

A bullet slammed into the ice beside her, and she hit the ground. Jake's feet pounded toward her, and she turned to see a look of deep concern on his face.

"They missed," she gasped. "I'm okay."

More bullets followed, somehow missing them. Jake grabbed her by the upper arm and dragged her to her feet, turning to fire. A yell of pain from one of the men suggested Jake had hit his mark. *Will backup come?* What would they do if Jake ran out of bullets? Throw icicles?

If she turned her ankle again, that wouldn't matter. She concentrated on the terrain in front of her, where the slipperiness of the glacier was surpassed only by the treacherous obstacles...

Megan Short is an Australian author of inspirational romantic suspense novels. She grew up in New Zealand, where her favorite activity was watching bumblebees and daydreaming. A screenwriter by trade, she has writing qualifications from UCLA and has won some screenwriting awards. Megan currently lives in Melbourne and loves learning new skills and meeting new people, many of whom make their way into her stories! She still spends too much time daydreaming and is a recovering chocoholic.

Books by Megan Short

Love Inspired Suspense

Alaskan Police Protector
Trapped on the Alaskan Glacier

Visit the Author Profile page at LoveInspired.com.

TRAPPED ON THE ALASKAN GLACIER

MEGAN SHORT

LOVE INSPIRED SUSPENSE
INSPIRATIONAL ROMANCE

MIX
Paper | Supporting responsible forestry
FSC
www.fsc.org
FSC® C021394

LOVE INSPIRED® SUSPENSE
INSPIRATIONAL ROMANCE

Recycling programs for this product may not exist in your area.

ISBN-13: 978-1-335-95755-9

Trapped on the Alaskan Glacier

Copyright © 2026 by Megan Short

Love Inspired
22 Adelaide St. West, 41st Floor
Toronto, Ontario M5H 4E3, Canada
www.LoveInspired.com

HarperCollins Publishers
Macken House, 39/40 Mayor Street Upper,
Dublin 1, D01 C9W8, Ireland
www.HarperCollins.com

Printed in Lithuania

Come unto me, all ye that labour and are heavy laden, and I will give you rest. Take my yoke upon you, and learn of me; for I am meek and lowly in heart: and ye shall find rest unto your souls.
—*Matthew* 11:28–29

Soli Deo gloria

ONE

"Your location has been compromised. A handler is on the way to extract you."

The caller from the US Marshals Service hung up, leaving Beth Ryder's heart to gallop into her throat. *How?* How had her location been compromised? She'd done everything her USMS handler, Tom Villani, had told her, and more. Changed her identity, including her appearance. Sidestepped into a new career. Broken contact with her family and all her friends. Disposed of every personal item. Canceled her social media profiles and even deleted her email account—fearful of ordering anything online. Moved to a small town, Cordova, on the east side of Prince William Sound, in southeast Alaska. Taken up new hobbies, dropping the old ones. Changed her accent and mannerisms. There was no conceivable similarity between the person she'd been three years ago and the person she'd become.

Beth's mind raced. *Anyone* discovering her location should be impossible! Blood rushed in her ears, and she leaned against the wall for support. The colorful posters crafted by the elementary school children that festooned the hallway linking the classrooms swirled in front of her like a rainbow whirlpool.

"Beth? Are you okay?" Felicity Davies, a fellow teacher,

placed a steadying hand on her shoulder. Her earthy-sweet perfume wafted toward Beth like patchouli-infused smelling salts. "Bad news?"

Beth drew a breath, relaxing the grip on the phone she clutched in her hand. "You could say that." She blinked, attempting to control the buzzing in her head. *Am I having a bad dream?*

"Anything I can do to help?" Concern lined Felicity's face and she gave Beth's shoulder a reassuring squeeze. The squeeze brought her back to reality, like a pinch. This was no dream. How Beth wished she could fall into Felicity's arms and cry on her shoulder. Not anymore. That would be suspiciously uncharacteristic for Beth Ryder.

"Thanks, it's fine." Beth forced a smile. "Just news I wasn't expecting."

"Okay, please let me know if I can help."

"I will, thanks, Felicity."

The teacher gave an understanding nod and walked down the hall, shoes squeaking like a flock of emperor geese, toward her classroom.

Beth pulled at the sleeve of her pastel cardigan. Her eyes glazed while she considered the situation. What should she do now? Had her new identity been compromised? She had to assume so. That's what Tom had said when he'd drilled her in the procedure. *Trust no one.* The thought of going through the laborious task of assuming another identity filled her with dread. She'd put everything into this one. Changing from Karina "Kari" Baumane to Elizabeth "Beth" Ryder had flipped her life upside down. She didn't love herself as Beth, but the persona had kept her safe from harm. No one grew close to Beth Ryder. No one could break down the barriers she'd built. Not only to protect herself, but also any unsuspecting new friend who might be used by those in the organized crime gang who wished to hunt her down. Beth massaged her temples, hoping the tension headache that threatened would subside. *That's all I need.*

She continued toward her classroom, and the sandwich and brownie she'd just eaten grew heavy in her stomach. Overeating had become the new normal for Beth, who needed something to offset the coldness she showed to those who might wish to grow close. She could make friendly acquaintances by bringing a steady stream of cookies, cakes, brownies, muffins, bars and more, to church, the school staff room, and any other occasion. Eating sweets was so uncharacteristic of her old self—the one who watched her weight and calorie counted like a Hollywood actress—that it had become an unexpected pleasure. Plump Beth Ryder, complete with curves. One change for the better.

With lunch break almost over, soon the composite class of K-3 students would race into the classroom for their afternoon lessons. Beth picked up her pace to reach class before the bell rang. She made it with a few minutes to spare, deposited her oversized handbag on her chair, then wrote the afternoon's spelling words on the whiteboard. Stepping back to check the words were written in straight columns, Beth gave herself a stern talking to. *Everything will be fine.* Tom had given her a plan for this scenario. After work, she would lay low at home until he could get there to her. He would take care of her.

Her racing heart calmed at the thought of his tanned, serious face with its deep hazel eyes and dark blond, wavy hair—clipped neatly to regulation length. The man had been a beacon of hope and comfort throughout this whole horrible ordeal. While the FBI had run the case against the Bulgarian organized crime gang—or "OCG" as they called it—boss, they hadn't been pleasant to work with. She'd been the sole witness to the raft of crimes with which he'd been charged. Because of her Bulgarian language skills, she'd been particularly valuable—the defense lawyers couldn't argue she'd misunderstood what she'd witnessed. The FBI's relentless questioning and pressure had worn her down until she'd agreed to testify. Only, her testimony had come at a great personal price. Her life would be in danger until every last loose end had been run down. Probably for the rest of her life.

Which was where Tom came in. As one of only a handful of witnesses eligible for the Witness Security Program run by the US Marshals Service, Beth had been assigned a handler. Tom had taken care of her relocation, settling her in and ensuring her security. At first, he'd been with her twenty-four seven. But soon, she'd settled in. Once the USMS was satisfied she'd be safe on her own, Tom had left. Beth's time spent with Tom had been enough to convince her he was the only one who could properly protect her from the threats from the OCG. She'd become even more convinced of this when she'd learned one of the OCG members was a US senator. She'd witnessed Petrov promote him within the OCG. Testifying against a sitting US senator complicated everything. Other unknown parties might want to silence her, and the danger increased. But it hadn't bothered Tom. Kind, sensible and strong, with a husky Chicago accent, he'd become her protector and safe harbor. She didn't know a lot about his personal life, except he was married, and he'd had a career as a marine raider before becoming a US marshal. But she didn't have to. All that mattered to Beth was his competence, and he had *that* in spades. Even with her identity compromised, and the Bulgarians after her, she'd be safe with Tom by her side.

The bell rang, snapping Beth out of her reverie. Children's

voices and footsteps running to line up outside the door signaled the time for focusing on her troubles had passed.

The afternoon dragged, and unlike usual, a lightness filled Beth when the final bell signaled the end of the day. Once the last child had been safely dispatched, Beth cleaned up the classroom, wondering when she'd next be back. If ever. The thought brought a heaviness to her chest. How she loved teaching a class of children. Much better than the live-in tutor and au pair roles she'd had in the past. That's what she'd been doing when she witnessed Kamen Petrov, leader of the Bulgarian OCG, order the killing of two men, and promote the man she now knew was a US senator to a higher position in the gang. She swallowed the lump in her throat. Petrov and the senator belonged in prison, and she needed to stay strong to see justice done. Even if that meant leaving this new home to avoid the men Petrov would send to kill her— the only witness. *Nothing lasts forever.* The mantra had kept her on track since this ordeal began.

"Miss Ryder, do you have a moment?" Mrs. Sutton, the principal, padded into the classroom, a frown creasing her brow. Rumor had it, as the most senior teacher, the sixty-something woman had been forced into the role when her predecessor left. Whatever her feelings might be, Beth had never noticed her being anything other than competent.

"Yes, Mrs. Sutton, I'm just finishing up." Beth cleaned her hands with a wet wipe and joined the principal, who'd sat at one of the small tables.

"I won't beat about the bush. Some parents have raised concerns about you."

Beth pursed her lips, her stomach tensing. "I'm sorry to hear that."

"Yes." Mrs. Sutton leaned forward. "They're unhappy

about your recent discussion on cyber safety. In particular, your negative opinion of social media."

A sigh escaped Beth's lips before she could stop it. She'd been asked to give a talk about social media during a recent parent-teacher night, and it had not gone well. Beth had given the opinion—she'd thought it uncontroversial—that images of children should never be posted on social media. To say it had been very poorly received would be an understatement. Only one parent had shown support—Rachel, the wife of a local police officer, and the only parent she could loosely count as a friend.

"My private opinion is that you're absolutely correct, and I'm raising it with you strictly as a formality. Can you refrain from repeating your opinion again?" Mrs. Sutton raised her eyebrows.

"Of course."

She smiled. "Fantastic. Consider the box ticked. No further action required." The principal stood to leave, then paused. "I'll be asking them—in such a way they cannot refuse—to take down the post."

Beth's stomach dropped. "Post?"

"One of the parents has posted about it on social media. She took a video of your talk—"

"Excuse me?" Beth's mouth gaped. "She took a video of *me* and posted it *online*?"

Mrs. Sutton's frown returned. "It seems so. They all post online, it's what this younger generation does. I'm surprised that you don't, honestly. It's quite refreshing to have a member of staff under the age of forty who doesn't spend lunch scrolling something or other."

Beth closed her eyes. Could a parent be the reason she had to be extracted from her new life? Surely, she wouldn't be recognizable, even from a video. Then again, with artificial intelligence technology, any images could be a problem. "You don't understand..." She stopped herself. What was the point? "I'm sorry, forget I said anything. I appreciate your support, Mrs. Sutton, I really do."

Beth's jaw clenched as she hurried along the hallway toward the parking lot. How frustrating she may have done this to herself. She should have made all parents surrender their phones when they'd entered the classroom.

Distracted, she stopped before the sliding doors to root around in her bag for her car keys. In May, the remaining chill in the air meant she didn't want to spend more time outdoors than she could help. *Why can I never find them?* A fingernail caught on the zipper of her purse and she gasped, hoping it wouldn't ruin her manicure. Carefully applied nail polish represented another thing her former self had never had to contend with. Finding her keys, she pulled them from the handbag. Then she bent her head to examine the damage to her nail and light flashed in her peripheral vision. The glass door shattered and a blast of air knocked her off her feet.

I thought I had more time.

Deputy US Marshal Jake Cruz surveyed the airport—a generous name for a landing strip—in Cordova, Alaska. He took a deep, satisfying breath of fresh, cold air. *Just like I remember it.* His first and last experience in Alaska had been blissful. Jake's childhood had been one of frequent moves to wherever the US Army posted his father. Spending sixth grade at Fort Wainwright, Fairbanks, had been his hands-down favorite. Hard to believe more than fifteen years had passed since he'd braved the bitter cold winter nights with his two older sisters and younger brother to watch the aurora borealis. He fondly remembered every single trip they'd taken during his father's leave, where they'd walked over glaciers and paddled their kayaks along rivers or in the ocean among the icebergs. The cold didn't bother him, and the unique wildlife had intrigued him, so he'd insisted on stopping whenever a bald eagle flew overhead—some requests more successful than others. When his father had been reassigned, Jake had considered staging a protest. Only the thought of the embarrassment his father would suffer—and the wrath that would rain down upon Jake as a consequence—had made him do nothing more than remain sullen on the plane to Arizona. While his dad had been assigned far and wide in the years to come, Fairbanks had been his one and only Alaska post.

When the USMS assigned Jake to this case, he took the first plane out of Chicago. Swinging his bag over his shoulder, he strode toward the waiting police cruiser. An officer and his K9—a cheerful-looking husky—stood nearby.

"Deputy US Marshal Jake Cruz." He held out his hand to the officer, whose Italian heritage was as obvious as his own Hispanic.

The officer smiled, his grip firm. "Officer Samuel Miller. Welcome to Cordova."

"Thanks."

The crackle of Miller's radio interrupted. "All units, we have a detonated car bomb at the elementary school. I repeat, a car bomb has been detonated at the elementary school. All units respond."

Jake's stomach dropped and he reached for the door to the cruiser. A bombing at his witness's place of work wasn't a coincidence. *Lord, please don't let her die.*

Officer Miller ushered the K9 into the car, and Jake slid into the front seat. He gave Jake a look that mirrored his prayer, then flipped on the lights and sirens, and pealed out of the parking lot. Jake swallowed, thankful Miller had a lead foot.

Less than five minutes later, Jake stepped out of the cruiser in the elementary school parking lot. A light misting of rain wet the smoke billowing from a destroyed hatchback. Two fire trucks shielded the scene from the public. One hosed down the adjacent cars, while the other worked on the charred shell of what Jake assumed used to be Beth's car.

"You go ahead and check on Beth. Looks like she wasn't… She'll be inside." Officer Miller's voice interrupted his assessment, and Jake looked toward the newly painted blue-and-sea-green building where the police officer had gestured. "Bruce, come." The dog followed his master toward the cordon.

Jake took his bag with him and paced toward the elementary school building. He had to find Beth. Hopefully whoever had detonated the bomb had not hung around, but he couldn't count on it. No one stood out as a Bulgarian assassin at first glance.

The smell of smoke and fire retardant filled the air, and several teachers milled around the school, white-faced. He bypassed them, scanning the area for a slight, blue-eyed Nordic blonde. Not finding her, he walked toward the building.

A shattered glass door greeted him, and he picked his way through the glass and into the hallway. A paramedic treated a Rubenesque woman with auburn ringlets, dressed in a pastel twinset, for minor facial cuts. She must've been near the door when the bomb detonated. He strode toward an older woman who exuded the confidence of someone in charge.

He held up the five-pointed star of his badge. "Deputy US Marshal Cruz. Could you tell me where Beth Ryder is, please?"

The woman regarded him with skepticism, her lips pursed. "She's behind you."

He turned. The paramedic was half a foot too tall to be Beth. *The redhead?* "Miss Ryder?" Her green eyes locked with his, and he saw it. Under the change of hair, the contact lenses, the weight and the clothes…his witness. He crouched down next to her, showing her his badge. "I'm Jake Cruz. You ready to get out of here?"

The paramedic stood, grabbing her medical bag. "She's good to go."

"Where's Tom?" Beth's brow creased. She peered toward the door as if Jake's colleague could appear at any moment.

"He's out with the flu. Don't worry, I've been in this job even longer than him. You're going to be fine."

He understood her hesitation. Reading the file on the plane over, he'd discovered Villani had been on the case since the start. Change could be hard for witnesses, especially those like Beth who were innocent victims rather than criminals.

Beth's eyes bulged and her face drained of color. "He's not coming?"

The older woman in charge stepped toward them, gaze dripping with suspicion. "You said you're from the US Marshals Service? What's this about?"

"Mrs. Sutton, I—" Beth swallowed, staring at the floor. "I—" Her eyes darted to Jake for guidance.

Mrs. Sutton raised an eyebrow. "Miss Ryder, are you in some kind of trouble? We're here to help."

Jake's shoulders relaxed. The woman had no idea of Beth Ryder's status as a protected witness, which meant Beth must have played things by the book. It answered one of the questions that troubled Jake—whether the compromise in Beth's cover had been a result of her confiding in the wrong people. As far as he knew, only the local police chief had been looped into the situation—and even then, no detail, just Beth's position as a protected witness. But with the current circumstances he must've informed other officers. Were they trustworthy?

"Miss Ryder isn't in any kind of trouble, she's assisting us. It'd help everyone involved if you'd minimize any speculation." Jake held out his hand and Beth took it. Hers felt soft and moderately clammy, and she smelled of rosewater.

Mrs. Sutton's eyes widened. "I don't think—"

"I need to get Miss Ryder to safety." He spoke with the authority that people usually didn't question.

Mrs. Sutton pursed her lips and stepped back to let them pass.

The USMS division office had arranged for the local police department to provide a civilian car while he stayed in town. The bombing had interrupted the smooth handover, and a young, uniformed officer waited in the parking lot next to the sedan.

Once he'd signed the paperwork and confirmed the situation with a call to his boss, Jake helped Beth into the car.

"Come on, let's get you home." Jake closed the door for Beth, checking for any suspicious activity and finding none. No doubt someone watched him from somewhere, but with the commotion of emergency services and bystanders, it was impossible to determine anything more. He'd already plotted the route to Beth's house—a roundabout route that would help him check for a tail. He drove sedately through the town and looped back to Beth's street. Nothing unusual so far.

Beth had remained silent since the few words she'd uttered to Mrs. Sutton. Jake had no idea whether to attribute that to her personality or shock. Suited him, he didn't need to field a barrage of questions while he navigated this unfamiliar, potentially hostile territory.

The unease in his gut made him pull to the curb several doors down from Beth's address. Beth licked her lips, he guessed from nervousness, and waited. She knew the drill, this wasn't her first safe house. Still, no point taking chances by leaving things unclear.

"I'll get out first and come around to you. I don't want you in the line of fire."

"Sure." She avoided eye contact when he held out his hand for her.

Jake walked Beth down the sidewalk, one hand on her arm, the other on his weapon. The muted blues and grays of the houses set against the occasional red stood out against the evergreen backdrop, reminding him of Fairbanks. While some of Beth's neighbors had shrubbery in their front yards, hers appeared relatively clear. The house was beautifully maintained, just like Beth. Security cameras peeked from under the shallow eaves and the front was shielded by a security door. Jake remained hyperalert as they approached Beth's house. Something didn't seem right.

A bullet whizzed past his head and he yanked Beth to the ground behind him, his gun raised. *Where did it come from?*

TWO

Jake spotted the flash from the muzzle of the firearm, then the next bullet sailed too close for comfort. A rifle. Came as a surprise they'd missed. The OCG usually hired professional assassins. Could this be an opportunistic local amateur? Shielding Beth with his body, he returned fire. He easily hit the assailant, who went down with a yell. Not dead.

Keeping his eyes on the assailant, who groaned and clutched his shoulder, he reached behind him for Beth. "You good?"

"I'm fine." Her voice shook as much as the cold little hand that grasped his.

"There may be others. Stay down and stay close." Head down, he hustled toward the assailant, checking the surrounds for others. The man had hit the ground at the corner of Beth's house. Jake's bullet had gone through his shoulder. He'd survive. With a clear line of sight down the side of Beth's house, it became clear no one else lay in wait.

Jake pulled some zip ties from his vest and secured the man's hands behind his back. The man cursed and spat. Beth's gasp reminded him this would be a shock for her. How different from other witnesses he'd protected. He'd have to remember to cut her some slack. Removing the bullets from the still-hot rifle, and piling them out of sight behind a flowerpot for the police to retrieve, he leaned the weapon against the house.

"He can't hurt you now. Stay down by the side of the house."

Beth did as he said, averting her eyes from the man.

He pulled his cell out and dialed the local PD. "This is Deputy US Marshal Cruz. I have a gunshot wound for you." Once he'd given the details to the dispatcher, she assured him help would arrive shortly.

Jake crouched to secure the man's ankles to Beth's balustrade with a zip tie. He'd disguised himself in fisherman's clothing. Riffling through his pockets, Jake found nothing that might identify him. They needed to get inside.

"You armed your alarm system when you left?"

"Mmm-hmm, yes." Beth remained crouched against the wall.

"Okay, let's go check inside. Can we get in round back?"

Beth nodded.

"Stay close." He shielded Beth between his body and the side of the house until they reached the backyard. The tremor in Beth's hand had lessened, and he gave it a squeeze before checking around the corner. Nothing. "Let's go."

The door led into the laundry, and he waited for Beth to unlock it while he stayed on the lookout. She fumbled the keys several times before the dead bolt slid back. Once safely inside, Jake dodged around the inconveniently placed laundry rack and waited for Beth to disarm the alarm system. He proceeded to clear each room, with Beth at his side, checking the access points. Nothing disturbed.

Every room of Beth's house looked and smelled like something from a vintage home décor magazine—all lacy doilies, potpourri and flowered prints. The only reason he even knew about such matters was half a lifetime spent with two excessively girly sisters, now military wives. He considered the incongruence of the fussy housekeeping to the scruffy, blond waif he'd read about in the WITSEC file. How had that woman morphed into the one he'd met today? Was it a mask she could remove, or had she permanently changed in the space of a few years?

They ended the house tour just as the police pulled up out front.

"Go pack a bag while I take care of this." Jake left Beth inside and shut the front door securely behind him.

"Miss Ryder's keeping us all busy today. Is she okay?" A young officer, wearing latex gloves, had already handcuffed the man, cut the zip tie and watched over him while some paramedics loaded him onto a gurney. He held the rifle.

"Yes, she's fine. Just inside." Jake looked the officer up and down. No threat there.

"What a relief. I'm Officer Jock O'Halloran. Miller—Officer Miller—is on his way. We just clocked off from the bomb site."

"Sorry to have to bring you back on duty."

O'Halloran shrugged. "Don't sweat it, we're all happy to help Miss Ryder."

"Have you seen this guy around before?" Jake's eyes tracked the man as the paramedics wheeled him toward the ambulance.

"Nope. But there's always an influx of fishermen after breakup. Lots of folks head north to earn some money."

Jake recalled the "breakup" O'Halloran referred to was the ice breaking up on the lakes and rivers when the warmer spring weather arrived. He imagined the ice breaking up on the local Eyak Lake might be a welcome relief after a long winter for the local population.

Another patrol vehicle pulled up and Officer Miller and his K9 stepped out to greet them. "Beth's okay?"

"She's fine." O'Halloran reached to hand the K9 a treat. The dog's tail wagged, and Jake could have sworn he smiled.

Jake needed to get back to Beth. He gestured to the evidence bag filled with bullets Officer O'Halloran handed to his colleague. "There may be my prints on those, I'm afraid. I didn't want to leave a loaded weapon out in the open."

"Better to be safe." Officer Miller scratched his K9 behind the ear.

"Thanks for your help. If you can hold him in custody for now, the FBI will be in touch to take him off your hands. They'll do the investigation. There's security camera footage that they'll need to access from across the road, and here."

"Leave it with us." Miller held out his hand and shook Jake's.

Jake followed the sound of a kettle boiling into the kitchen. Beth's handbag rested on the kitchen table and she'd removed her shoes.

He raised his eyebrows. "What are you doing? Pack a bag. Let's get out of here."

Beth turned to face him, her arms crossed in front of her. "No. I'm not going anywhere."

"What?" Jake normally prided himself on his ability to mask any surprise that came his way. Not this time. He stepped back, his mouth gaping.

"I said, I'm not going anywhere. You can protect me here."

"That's not an option. My mission is to extract you."

Beth reached for a bone china cup and saucer adorned with pink roses. "Too bad. You've just disabled the guy Petrov sent. I can leave once Tom gets here. Doesn't take more than a week to recover from the flu, does it? By then the elementary school will have time to find my replacement too."

Tom? Jake's blood pressure rose. Was she in shock, or would this be a problem? He hadn't read anything out of the ordinary in her file. Seemed like a stock-standard WITSEC witness, albeit a noncriminal, which was unusual. Also unusual was the extreme makeover. Hopefully, he could reason her out of this attitude. Get her to cooperate with him.

Beth laid out a second cup and saucer, dangled an Earl Grey teabag into the first and reached for a cookie jar. "Tea or coffee?"

Crossing his arms, Jake shook his head. "You're not staying here, Miss Ryder. We need to move locations, then jump on the next plane to Anchorage."

Beth ignored him, pouring boiling water over the teabag. The aroma of bergamot wafted toward him. "You look like a coffee guy to me." She reached for a tin of instant. "I don't drink coffee myself. I just keep this on hand for guests."

Jake considered whether he would have to handcuff her and drag her to the airport by force. Not a good option. He'd have to negotiate, which wouldn't be a problem if he were any good at it. His ex-fiancée had hammered that fact home. One of the many criticisms she'd hurled at him when they'd parted ways. *Don't think about her.* Easier said than done. Jake rubbed his forehead. How long could he keep Beth Ryder safe in her house? Probably a while. He'd been in siege situations before. But he would never willingly manufacture one, which is what remaining here would be. Rifle Guy's failure to check in would cause the OCG to put another hit man on the next plane. Would one last night in her own bed get her to see sense in the cold light of morning? Maybe. When she realized leaving the house to teach wasn't an option, and that Tom wasn't coming, that might focus her mind.

Instant coffee was a bridge too far, though. "Thanks, but I'd rather a Coke if you have it?" He'd have to stay up tonight; the caffeine would help.

"Oh, sure." Beth opened the fridge and pulled a can of Coke from the top shelf. "You want ice?"

"No, I'm good, thanks."

She poured his Coke into a tall crystal glass and handed it to him.

"Thanks." He took a sip and the harsh, sugary fizz helped more than expected.

Beth perched at the table, cradling the cup of tea and watched him. Her artificially green eyes locked with his. "We're staying here?" The way she asked suggested her certainty from earlier had either been a façade, or shock, as he'd suspected.

"For tonight, at least. There's only one commercial flight out each day and it's left already."

She sighed. "Good. I'll fix dinner."

Several hours later, they'd eaten a surprisingly delicious chicken dinner, and Beth had slipped off to bed.

Jake called in to update his boss on the situation.

"I don't like it, Cruz. You need to get her out of there. I can organize a charter plane if necessary. The FBI has the budget." The low rumble of Supervisory Deputy United States Marshal Bob Forsyth's elite, boarding-school-educated voice echoed down the line. Though barely a year older than Jake, the man had an aura of authority that had catapulted him up the chain of command.

"Short of slinging her over my shoulder and dragging her onto the plane, there's no way that's going to happen before the morning, sir."

"Humph. Use your charm, Cruz. If you dig deep enough, there must be some somewhere."

"Yes, sir. I'll keep you updated." Jake ended the call. His boss knew very well that charm happened to be another gift the Lord had *not* given Jake. With even an ounce of charm, maybe things would've turned out differently. In many areas of his life. His mind returned to his ex-fiancée, and he rubbed his hands over his scalp. *Nope, don't go there.* Releasing the breath he didn't know he'd been holding, he checked his watch. A little over twelve hours before the next flight left. He'd convince Beth to get on it one way or another.

She presented him with a bit of a conundrum. Her impressive self-discipline to stick to a new identity then astonishingly irrational behavior when she found her life in danger. No matter, he'd keep her safe. *That* he was good at.

Hours later, as Jake patrolled the front of Beth's house, his phone buzzed.

Forsyth again. "The FBI's been in touch. They've had information about an assassin on a commercial flight out of Seattle, but we have no information on his identity. It's a full flight, so it will take time to vet the passengers. Safer to get out of there."

"Any description at all?"

"None. You should avoid the airport, though. If someone's meeting him, they'll go after the witness. You have two hours."

Jake's pulse quickened. There were only two ways in or out of Cordova, and with the airport option gone, they'd have to travel by sea. He'd already checked their options while he'd kept watch at Beth's house. "The next ferry leaves at zero five hundred. We'll be on it."

"Good plan. Keep me updated."

If another gang member had already made it into Cordova, he needed to keep his eyes open.

* * *

Beth woke in the middle of a happy dream when the light flicked on. She threw her arm over her face, wishing away the glare.

"Miss Ryder, we have to go."

The abrasive voice snapped her awake properly. Beth squinted toward the towering form of the US marshal who stood in the frame of her doorway. Not Tom. She set her jaw. This guy had none of Tom's finesse, and probably a fraction of his talent. Yet she had to rely on him for her safety. Would they even make it out of Cordova alive? How she'd hoped that staying here would allow Tom the time to recover and reach her. How much safer she'd feel if he were here.

Swallowing down the lump that formed in her throat, she blinked, her eyes focusing on Deputy Jake Cruz. Tall, probably six feet. Hispanic. A clipped mustache set against the five-o'clock shadow of his face and shaved head. His posture stiff; matching his stern expression. Urgh. He might be handsome if it weren't for that permanent scowl.

"Now." His tone sounded the same as that he'd used on Mrs. Sutton yesterday. Authority expecting compliance. He probably had a good reason to get her up like this, but he didn't have to be so rude. Beth rubbed her eyes. If that was the way he wanted it, she wouldn't go out of her way to be friendly either.

"Hold your horses." Her voice came out in a sleepy croak and she rolled over, forcing her body up to a sitting position. "What's the rush?" She glanced at the clock and gasped. "It's only—"

"Sixteen minutes past four. Yes, I'm aware. We should've been lining up on the ferry ramp sixteen minutes ago." The clipped words, delivered at a volume slightly higher than natural for the early hour, ended with a slight grunt for emphasis.

"Okay, okay. I need to get dressed." Something must have happened. Jake might be a prickly, unfeeling man, but he'd have been trained by the same people who'd trained Tom. If he said they had to get on that ferry at the last minute, he'd have a good reason.

"You've got four minutes." He closed the door behind him.

Beth dressed hurriedly, using a quick trip to the bathroom to splash cold water on her face and grab her bug out bag—another poignant reminder of Tom, who'd helped her decide what to pack in it. Her mind returned to the day he'd explained the purpose of the bag—"BOB" as he'd referred to it. He had one of his own at home, in case of emergency. *Everyone should be prepared,* he'd said. Beth had agreed completely, listening attentively to everything he'd said. She remembered every word, including the importance of energy bars and toothpaste. Vowing to put his teachings to use, she pressed the contact lenses onto her eyes and blinked. She'd focus on staying alive, just like he'd shown her. With twenty seconds to spare, Beth rushed past Jake to the kitchen and filled another bag with baked goods. No need to rely on the "ferry food" if she could help it.

"I'm ready."

Jake gave a curt nod and took her bag. Beth curbed her disappointment at his underreaction—Tom would've said something encouraging about her impressive haste. *Tom isn't here. Jake's doing his job.*

They left through the back door and retraced their steps to the car through frosty grass, which crunched underfoot. Jake's head twisted from side to side, and he kept his hand firmly on her triceps. What he hoped to see remained a mystery—any assailant lying in wait would have a tough

time seeing them in return. Dense fog had settled overnight and obscured all but a few yards ahead, including
her usual view of the harbor. The low, piercing calls of the
glaucous-winged gulls brought her some comfort. No doubt
they greeted the nearby fishermen, including the fathers of
some of her elementary students. Beth considered their fu-
tures as Jake checked the car, she assumed for explosives
or maybe trackers.

Touching the healing cuts on her face, she shivered. Jake's
manner might be brusque, but he hadn't hesitated to protect
her. He couldn't protect the children, though. What if one
of them had been standing near the car? While she hadn't
been speaking out of turn when she'd mentioned the lack
of substitute teachers, maybe *no* teacher was better than a
risky one. Although, they wouldn't be without a teacher.
Mrs. Sutton would have to teach them until she found a replacement. The children wouldn't enjoy that—they considered Mrs. Sutton a "stern teacher." Couldn't be helped. The
idea of not saying goodbye to her students left a dullness in
her chest that she couldn't lift.

How she wished this wasn't happening. That the life she'd
built could withstand an errant social media post.

Evidently satisfied the car was safe, Jake held the door
open. Joining her in the front seat, he finally spoke. "We're
taking the ferry from Cordova to Whittier. We'll drive to
the USMS Anchorage division office. You'll be safe there."

"Okay." What else could she say? The plan wasn't ne-
gotiable.

En route, Jake glanced in his mirror frequently, his jaw
tense. They approached the ferry terminal and his eyes
darted around as they joined the end of the last vehicle waiting line. Yellow-painted stripes marked out the five parallel
lanes on the asphalt jetty, making for an orderly entry to the

vessel's starboard. The first three lanes had already boarded by the time they arrived. Pedestrians with backpacks and duffel bags walked up a steel catwalk alongside the stream of cars. The row dwindled as the fourth line of vehicles edged toward the ferry. Soon it would be their turn.

As their line began to roll, Jake grabbed her shoulder and pushed her toward the foot well. "Stay down."

Beth clutched her knees as Jake slammed the gearshift into Park and leaped from the car.

Two bullets smashed the window above Beth's head before Jake returned fire. A man's cry of pain hit Beth right in the gut. There was a thud and a curse.

Is Jake hit?

THREE

A woman screamed, and Beth's stomach churned. Calls from the startled kittiwakes and gulls fleeing added to the cacophony. She'd be screaming, too, if her breath would come back. This was the second time in two days she'd been showered with glass, and the cuts on her face still stung. The shattered window gave her no protection from the commotion. Some yells came from Jake's direction, and Beth risked a peep through the window. Jake had grabbed the man, who tried to turn his gun back on the marshal.

"US Marshal! Drop your weapon! On the ground! On the ground, now!" The thunderous authority of Jake's voice made Beth recoil. At least he seemed okay. Maybe he hadn't been hit by a bullet. "Hands behind your head!"

Beth shrank toward the floor of the car. A body slamming onto the hood of the sedan startled her and she reflexively jerked up, bumping her head on the dash. She rubbed her scalp and stared. Jake had zip-tied a man's—presumably the shooter's—hands behind him. He had one hand firmly on the shooter's neck, holding him down as he struggled and spewed such colorful language that Beth blushed. Beth had a good view of the greasy, dark waves, thankful his face was turned away from hers. She shuddered, and some glass dislodged from her curls, falling onto her lap. How many shards had made it down the back of her top? No way she'd leave the vehicle to shake it out. Jake checked around him, while he dialed his cell phone.

"Assistance needed at the Cordova ferry terminal. One suspect in custody. He's suffered a bullet wound to the hip. Thanks." He ended the call and gestured for the ferry terminal agent to approach them.

The man, decked out in an orange safety vest and navy-blue jacket and beanie, regarded Jake with a mixture of respect and fear. Onlookers gaped and the line stalled.

Jake introduced himself then asked, "Have you checked incoming passengers for weapons?"

"Yes, we screen for weapons on all incoming passengers. They can bring weapons on board, but those need to be stowed, with the ammunition stored separately." The agent averted his eyes from the man in custody.

"Any way someone has snuck on a loaded weapon?"

The ferry terminal agent shook his head. "We're careful, sir."

Jake glanced over his shoulder, and Beth followed his gaze to the patrol vehicle bypassing the waiting line, blue and red lights strobing through the fog.

The shooter struggled again. "My leg!" Another colorful stream of language followed.

"That's enough." Jake wrenched him to his feet and dragged him toward the police vehicle, which had pulled up a few feet from them.

Officers Samuel Miller and Jock O'Halloran, with K9 Bruce in tow, climbed out. Beth liked the officers, they'd become as much friends as she'd allowed them to be, although she'd like to be much closer to Samuel's wife, Rachel, whose adorable niece, Katie, attended Beth's K-3 class. Perhaps now they'd understand why she'd kept them at arm's length.

"Thanks for getting here so quick." Jake passed the man to Officer O'Halloran.

The young officer grinned. "No problem, although you're filling up our holding cells."

Jake gave what might pass for a grin—a slight break in his scowl. "No harm giving the FBI a follow-up call. I expect they'll pick him up along with the other guy shortly. There are plenty of witnesses, and I'll send through my report when we reach Anchorage."

The ferry terminal agent returned to his duties and the line progressed, leaving a large gap in front of Jake's car. Beth glanced at the clock. They wouldn't leave on time at this rate.

Samuel shook Jake's hand. "Thanks. You need any assistance?"

"How's the security on this ferry?" Jake lowered his voice.

"Security is pretty good, but it's not airport security. We can do a full check if you want?"

He glanced at Bruce. "Is your K9 trained in explosives detection?"

Beth swallowed heavily. Explosives detection? Bombing her car was one thing, but did Jake truly believe the OCG would bomb a ferry with hundreds of innocent people on board? No way she'd put people in danger for her sake. She bit her lip.

"No, he's strictly patrol these days. We don't usually get much call for explosives here in Cordova."

"In that case, we'll have to pass. The ferry's late enough as it is." Jake glanced at Beth then back to Samuel.

"Okay, we'll stay here until you depart. The paramedics can treat the prisoner while we wait. I'll call you if we see anything suspicious." Samuel patted his side to bring Bruce to heel.

"Thanks." Jake scratched the husky behind the ear. "You don't happen to have a search mirror with you?"

"Afraid not, sorry. They may have one on board, just ask one of the deck officers." Samuel peered in through the smashed window to Beth. "How're you doing?"

Beth forced a smile. "I'm okay, thanks. Say hi to Rachel." How she wished there was time to thank Rachel for her support with the social media talk. Maybe if she returned to Cordova one day…

"Will do. Take care." He gestured for Bruce to follow him.

Jake returned to the car, put it into gear, then turned to her. "Are you okay?" His eyes searched hers, and for a moment she wondered if there were some human feelings in there. He reached toward her face and picked some glass out of her hair. Then he raised his eyebrows. "Any injuries?"

Nothing more than a package to be delivered safely. "No, I'm fine." *At least I know where I stand.* She swallowed. "I don't want to board the ferry if there's a chance they'll detonate another bomb. There are too many innocent people."

Jake gave her a hard stare. "I won't let that happen."

Within ten minutes, their vehicle had boarded and Jake had parked them below deck. Beth's chest grew tight when Jake insisted they stay in the car until he could be sure everyone had exited the vehicle storage area. The brightly lit, cavernous space had white walls and ceiling, with pipes and conduit exposed overhead, and a painted deck that had been separated into several lanes marked with yellow lines. SUVs, small trucks, cars and motorbikes packed the area. Many of the SUVs had recreational equipment like canoes and bicycles strapped to roof racks. If anyone wanted to conceal an explosive, they had plenty of nooks and crannies to do so. Jake couldn't possibly look everywhere.

"I know where to look," he'd remarked when he sourced

a mirror from one of the deck officers. Apparently, the deck officer was happy for him to inspect the vehicles once the passengers had moved on deck. Diesel fumes, brine and other undistinguishable, unpleasant odors assaulted her senses through the window cavity. Their car was parked at the end corner of the space, with the ramp at their rear. No one could hide behind them without Jake seeing.

"Can we go out on deck soon, please?" Her voice wobbled as seasickness kicked in. No windows in the vehicle deck left no horizon to focus on, although perhaps there wouldn't be anyway with the fog.

A grunt emanated from Jake's throat and his eyes flicked around the area. A grunt wasn't a comment either way. *Would* he make her stay here much longer? She sure hoped not.

The ferry's engines growled and the boat chugged away from the dock. Most of the passengers had left their vehicles, with some stragglers appeasing the barks and yowls of their pets. Once they'd left, Beth turned to Jake and fixed him with a pleading stare she hoped he couldn't refuse.

"I need to use the rest room."

"Already?" His baffled tone did not help her mood.

"Yes."

He grunted again, seemingly thinking things through. "You'll have to hold it while I inspect the area."

"Are you serious?"

"Wait here." Jake opened the door and stepped away from the car, mirror in hand. He walked along the line of vehicles, checking inside each with a flashlight he'd pulled from his vest and underneath with the mirror. He constantly glanced over his shoulder at her, although she wasn't sure how anyone could approach their car given Jake stood between her and the only exits.

After what felt like forever, he returned. "Come on." Jake

reached into the back seat and retrieved their bags, making her stay between him and the solid wall until they reached the nearest bathroom. He cleared the cubicle before allowing her to enter.

Catching a glimpse of her reflection in the mirror, Beth startled. Oh no, this would not do at all. She carefully fixed her hair and makeup, adjusting her outfit until she looked like Beth Ryder—not a hair out of place, nor a crease in her clothing. She only purchased clothes that were crease-resistant these days, so a quick brush usually worked. Thankfully the glass hadn't made it down the back of her neck, instead trapping itself in the collar of her blouse. Her outfit wouldn't get blood on it like the last one had. The thermals she'd worn—as recommended by Tom: *they dry quick and keep you warm*—chafed a little under her outer clothes. At least she wouldn't freeze out on the deck.

Seasickness kicked in properly and her stomach gave an ominous gurgle. She leaned over the sink, hoping it wouldn't last the entire twelve hours. Preferring any other mode of transport, she'd never been much of a sailor. Hopefully, Jake would let her out on deck shortly.

When Beth left the bathroom, stomach swirling, she found Jake leaning against the wall, staring at every passenger who passed.

He escorted her to the middle of the cafeteria without a word. Beth fixed her eyes on the shoreline. The mountains remained obscured by fog. She imagined the clear day on which she'd seen Orca Inlet for the first time. Her shoulders drooped. Would this be her last memory of the place she'd believed could be her forever home? Foggy nothingness?

Jake dumped her bag and the food she'd packed on the table in front of them and gestured for her to sit. She obliged, and his hand reached for a gold cross he wore on a chain around his neck. The gesture reminded her that she'd miss church today. Sundays had become a welcome routine in her life in Cordova, and Beth would miss the time with her church. While she wasn't particularly religious, the rituals and the knowledge that God existed made all of this less meaningless.

She realized she'd been staring at Jake's hand when he moved it. Could he be thinking about church too? Where did he even live? Not like she'd ask. And that was the problem. They couldn't keep this up for twelve hours, or however long it took to get her to Anchorage. Did he have a plan for when she got there? It didn't bear thinking about. Beth sighed. Maybe they could pass the time with some kind of activity? She'd brought a card game and a book, but neither appealed, especially as each required her to take her eyes off the horizon. With Jake's silence, not to mention her current state of mind, she might go crazy. Her stomach might have her visiting the bathroom all too soon. Maybe she should close her eyes after all.

She let out a deep sigh and her gaze lingered on the bag of food. They hadn't had breakfast, and dinner felt like a long time ago. Maybe she could partly blame low blood sugar for the nausea. Reaching for the bag, she pulled out her favorite comfort food—homemade chocolate-chunk brownies. Her mouth watered. This should take her mind off things for a bit. Opening up the box, she offered one to Jake.

He licked his lips. "No, thank you."

"Suit yourself." Beth took the largest one and started munching. The gooey perfection helped her to relax, and her stomach roiled a little less. She considered Jake, whose eyes roved around the cafeteria without ceasing. What a strange man. Obviously hungry yet refusing food. Everyone loved her brownies. Another strike against Jake. *The man doesn't have to eat your food, cut him some slack.* She had to make the best of it, and that wouldn't happen if she kept sniping at him in her mind.

She took another bite, but it didn't help. The smell of coffee and fried food became stifling. Beth returned the half-eaten brownie to the container and snapped the lid back on. She quickly fixed her lipstick. "I need some air."

Jake appraised her for a moment. The look in his eyes made her wonder whether he was considering zip-tying her in place. He certainly seemed to have an endless supply of restraints in that vest of his. Then he took a deep breath and exhaled. "Okay. But you need to stay with me at all times. No wandering off. Agreed?"

Easy to agree to that. Maybe she'd misjudged him. Or maybe they really were safe on this ferry after all. "Yes, sir."

He raised his eyebrows at the "sir," then held out his hand to help her up from her chair. "Come on."

Jake couldn't get the blue of Beth's eyes out of his head. The color of a kingfisher's iridescent feathers, almost teal, they'd stunned him when she'd woken, only to be hidden moments later behind those disappointing green contact lenses. He'd almost told her the charade had become futile. If the OCG had found her, they also knew what she looked like now. But such a comment would be unprofessional and uncalled for. Her appearance was her business. And she sure took it seriously. He'd lost count of the number of times she'd primped her hair and reapplied her makeup since they'd boarded the ferry. To call her "high maintenance" would be the understatement of the decade. Not his kind of woman at all. But those eyes… They could become a distraction. Perhaps the contacts were a good idea after all.

He wrapped his arm around her shoulder and they made

their way through the cafeteria toward the main deck, checking as he went. Nothing stood out, but he didn't plan to take any chances. The ferry appeared relatively full for May, and an assailant could blend into the crowd.

"Glad the sun's makin' an appearance." Two women approached them. He guessed both were in their mid-sixties, probably from the Southwest. Both were decked out in brightly colored ski jackets and stocking caps, identical cups of coffee in hand.

"Still feels like an ice bath," the other woman replied. Seeing Jake and Beth, they stopped. "Hi there, you two lovebirds on your honeymoon? We've met three honeymooning couples already this trip."

Beth pursed her lips. The companions giggled, shared a knowing glance, then smiled at them expectantly.

Jake gave them a wink, sure that honeymoons were the last thing on Beth's mind. "Just getting out for some air. I see the fog has lifted."

"Some. Mind you snuggle up and stay warm now." The woman returned Jake's wink, and he gently guided Beth to the side to let them by.

Jake took Beth's hand and gave it a squeeze. "You doing okay?" Her color seemed a little off. The shock of yesterday's bombing and then the intensity of two shootouts must be taking a toll on her.

She turned away. "I feel sick."

"Seasick? I can get you some medication if you need it."

Beth exhaled. "I just need some air."

Jake guided her out onto the deck, ensuring his body remained between her and the other passengers. Most were preoccupied taking photos and enjoying the view through the slowly dispersing fog. He spotted a couple canoodling—presumably one of the honeymooners. A few tourists had pulled the white-plastic deck chairs into position near the painted-white metal railings and were wrapped in blankets or sleeping bags. A young mom fussed over her toddler, who kept pulling off his hat and throwing it to the deck, while his older sister beamed at their dad who took photos of the scene.

Several ropes were hung on the walls, along with an ax. All possible weapons. He moved Beth into the middle of the deck—didn't want her anywhere near the water—and gestured for her to sit on a vacant deck chair. The thin blanket he'd snagged from inside wouldn't provide much warmth. Better than nothing. He wrapped it over her shoulders.

"Feeling any better?"

She sniffed then stared into the distance. "I'll survive." Thankfully the color had returned to her cheeks.

Jake stood guard and concentrated on the surrounds. No one appeared conspicuous, even though his gut instinct alerted him to something. His gut had served him well over the years. *They must be somewhere, but where?* He'd give Beth a few minutes, then they could return to the cafeteria. Being outside made him nervous. The longer they stayed in one place, the more time someone had to plan something, and he hoped to avoid any outdoor confrontation so close to a freezing body of water. Especially if he had to arrest someone—they'd been on the water four hours, and they'd reach the next stop, Valdez, in two more. Then they'd remain on the ferry until Whittier, another six hours. Plenty of time for the OCG to get someone on the ground. The check of the vehicle deck had turned up nothing, thankfully. Someone from the OCG would be driving a car rather than a motorhome, and between the SUVs with kayaks on their roofs and family sedans, nothing had stood out. Most likely anyone from the OCG would be a pedestrian passenger. Hopefully that meant the bomb had been a one-off that required a little more planning than the shootings.

Nothing more I can do now. Jake took in the awe-inspiring scenery, even as he kept up his guard. No different to the memories from sixth grade. Jagged mountains rose from the moraines left by glaciers thousands of years earlier, shrouded in mist. How he'd missed Alaska. The ferry passed iridescent-blue icebergs with small flocks of pelagic cormorants perched on top. The mewing call of herring gulls approached, and the birds circled around through the smoke-like clouds toward the rocky shores blanketed with vegetation. The dewiness of the fog had been replaced with a cold freshness that made Jake glad of his heavy coat and beanie. He did not want to stay out here longer than absolutely necessary, especially when he didn't know where a potential assailant waited.

"Are you ready to get back inside?"

Beth frowned. "We just got out here, what's the rush?"

"It's not safe out in the open. I want you below deck."

"Don't you think it's safer here? Look at all these people. I don't think anyone's going to try and attack me in front of them. There's nowhere for them to go afterward."

She had a point, but the truth was, Jake didn't like the lack of control in this open space. He had no guarantee an assailant would act rationally. Whatever the OCG had hanging over their foot soldiers could be more gruesome than getting arrested or shot.

"No. I'll give you ten more minutes and then we need to get back inside."

Something made Jake turn his head to the left. A man kept glancing at Beth then speaking into his cell phone. Jake's chest tingled, and he took a deep breath. His hand instinctively went to his weapon—*he'd* been allowed to hold on to it after flashing his badge. He appraised the man, quickly positioning himself so that no harm could come to Beth if the man pulled a weapon of his own. Momentarily meeting Jake's gaze, the man hustled along the port deck away from them. This left Jake in no doubt that they were under surveillance. He needed to find out more. Were there others on the ferry? Had the man reported to someone else on board or had he called someone on shore? Jake placed his hand on Beth's shoulder.

"Time to go back inside."

She licked her lips. "You said ten minutes. We've barely had two." The tone of her voice held unease rather than annoyance. Had she spotted the man too? Seemed unlikely; she'd been staring in the opposite direction.

"Now, Miss Ryder."

Beth huffed as she stood, allowing him to guide her toward the interior. The man would've had time to double back by now, but Jake doubted he'd be dumb enough to do that yet. He would've heard about his colleagues and their gunshot wounds. More likely he'd bide his time and try to attack Beth when Jake let his guard down. That wasn't going to happen.

Jake ushered Beth into the cafeteria and checked for the man. The only people inside were regular passengers eating breakfast. He directed Beth into the same chair, the one facing the window. That should help with the seasickness, and he could push her under the table if anything happened.

He considered their options. At present, they were sitting ducks. The OCG's man knew where they were and could probably work out their plans to travel from Whittier to Anchorage. Their best option was to disembark at Valdez and go overland to Anchorage. But if they waited until the ferry docked, it would give the man an opportunity to follow them and guess their change of plan. Or worse, he could use the confusion of passengers disembarking and boarding to attack.

How am I going to get out of this one?

FOUR

Kayaks. During his search of the vehicle parking area, Jake had spotted several one- and two-man vessels atop roof racks. If he could borrow one and launch it over the side before they reached Valdez, he and Beth could slip away unnoticed. Only, they'd have to abandon their car. How would they make it to Anchorage then? There wasn't much time to decide, they'd be docking in half an hour. The man hadn't made an appearance again, which made Jake nervous.

With Beth's face returning to its seasick pallor, he hadn't been able to take her with him and find out more. Too bad, they needed to get off the ferry soon.

"Let's go."

Beth didn't hesitate, standing and allowing him to lead her out of the cafeteria. But when they headed below deck rather than out into the fresh air, she stopped. "Where are we going?" Her voice wobbled.

He leaned in so no one else would hear. "We're getting off the ferry. Could you please trust me without a discussion?"

"Fine." Beth pressed her lips together.

He directed her toward the vehicle deck, alert to the fact the man may be lying in wait for them.

Instead, a young deckhand stopped them. "You're not allowed down here for another ten minutes."

Jake flashed his badge. "I'm here on official business."

The deckhand gave him a skeptical frown. "Official business with the vehicles? I don't think so. I'm going to need to contact my supervisor."

Beth clutched her stomach. "I think I'm going to be sick."

Impressed with her improvisation, Jake seized on the opportunity. "I'm sure you don't want to be cleaning up after… well, that."

Glowering, the deckhand reached for a nearby bucket and handed it to Beth. "Here, ma'am, you can use this. Now, I'm calling my supervisor." He reached for his radio, and Beth heaved into the bucket. Alarmed, he glanced between Jake and Beth.

Jake raised his eyebrows and shrugged while he rubbed Beth's back. "Thanks for the bucket. We ran out of seasickness medication. It's in the car."

The deckhand pursed his lips. "You're still not supposed to be down here. My job is security, and I take it seriously. You should understand that."

"You're doing a great job. Have you seen anyone else enter the area?"

"No, there's no one here."

Jake held the bucket while Beth wiped her mouth with a tissue. "You checked everywhere?"

"Yeah. It's my job. I do my security rounds, and I stand watch."

While grateful the young man seemed thorough, Jake wasn't sure how they were going to grab a kayak out from under his nose.

Beth looked miserable and gave a slight sob. The sour smell of the bucket filled the air.

The deckhand rubbed his nose. "Where's your vehicle?"

Jake pointed to their sedan down at the back of the vault-like vehicle parking area.

"You can go get your medication, okay?"

"Thanks. Come on." Jake walked toward the car, keeping Beth close. She clutched the bucket for dear life.

They neared the vehicle, and Beth's face drooped. "What are we doing? I don't think my stomach can take much more of this." The bright lighting against the whitewashed walls revealed her slightly green tinge.

"You're going to be okay. This will be over soon."

Then the deckhand cried out and slumped to the ground. Jake's muscles tightened in readiness. That explained where the man had gotten to. The lights went out and booted feet pounded between the lines of vehicles, heading in their direction.

Jake dropped their bags, pushed Beth to the ground next to the car wheel, upsetting the bucket, and grabbed his gun. Drawing a deep breath, he crouched and peered through the car's window, hoping his eyes would adjust to the light from emergency signs soon. Where was the man? And what had he done to the deckhand? Hopefully the young man wouldn't suffer any permanent damage. *Lord, please help him. And us.*

"We need to keep moving," he whispered into Beth's ear. He threw their bags through the smashed car window, placed his hand on Beth's shoulder and guided her around the back of the car, away from the last-known position of the assailant. As his eyes adjusted, Jake made out the looming shapes of familiar vehicles. He'd checked each and every one earlier, and he remembered roughly the locations and layout. The footsteps had quietened. Perhaps the man had realized the noise announced his location. Maybe he'd doubled back. No point second-guessing. They needed to stay on mission. Grab a kayak and get out of there.

They'd made it halfway along the row of vehicles before the sound of a clatter, a curse and the thud of someone falling over echoed behind them.

Jake pushed Beth down. "Stay here." He raced to where the noise had come from and found the man on the ground, rubbing his shoulder. He'd tripped over Beth's bucket. What were the chances? *Thanks, Lord.*

He pointed the gun at the man's head. "Hands behind your head. Now."

The guy reached for his weapon, and Jake fired, hitting him in the shoulder. Crying out, the man grabbed the wound.

Jake skirted the mess and, ignoring the cries and protests, yanked the man onto his stomach. He grabbed a zip tie from his vest and bound the man's hands behind his back. "The more you struggle, the worse it'll hurt." He retrieved the man's cell phone, threw it into a nearby dinghy, then dragged him behind a car so he'd be obscured from view. No need to advertise what had just happened, and if he could stop the guy from seeing Jake drag a kayak out of the hold, that'd be even better. Reaching into the car, he grabbed their bags.

Beth stayed huddled in the same position he'd left her, tears staining her face. She quickly wiped them away and sniffed.

"Let's get out of here. Are you okay to take these?"

She reached out and he saddled her with her bags and his. They were awkward for her, but it couldn't be helped if he was to maneuver a tandem kayak and paddles up to the deck.

The deckhand remained unconscious, but his vitals seemed okay. Someone would find him soon. Jake dragged the kayak up onto the starboard deck, checking for other passengers. To his surprise, no one was around. *What's happening?* He placed the kayak on the deck and grabbed the bags from Beth, securing them to the stern. Tucking the paddles into the cockpit, he considered their options. He could lower the kayak using one of the many ropes, but that took time. Getting him and Beth over safely and quickly without attracting attention posed the challenge.

"Look!" Beth's voice cut through his thoughts. She'd moved along the deck toward the bow and pointed through the window to the crowd of passengers, all of whom appeared to be congregated on the starboard side. "I think it's a whale!"

Jake's heart warmed. Not because of the humpback that had decided to put on a show near Port Valdez, but the opportunity they now had to get away without any witnesses. Grabbing two life jackets, he secured one to himself before helping Beth into hers. At that moment, the whale breeched.

He picked up the kayak, dropped it over the port side, then grabbed Beth and looked her in the eyes. *Better she doesn't know.* "Hold your breath."

Her confusion turned to horror when he pulled her over the side of the ferry, dropping them into the freezing water below.

Beth's body seized the moment the bone-stabbing cold encased her. *What on earth...?* Had Jake just thrown them overboard? She gasped, inhaling a mouthful of salt water then coughing and spluttering. Jake grasped her arm and kicked toward the kayak, using his free hand to grab hold of it. They were going to freeze to death by the time they reached the shore. And for what? So the man, who Jake had already taken care of, wouldn't get them? The reasoning seemed bizarre.

Jake boosted her into the front seat of the kayak, and she dodged the paddles as he climbed in behind her and pulled them out. "Think you can paddle?"

"I can barely feel my hands! What's wrong with you?

Hold your breath. Seriously?" The words spilled out before she could stop them.

The grunt behind her could be all the response she'd get. Jake passed her the second paddle, which she rested across the sides of the kayak. No way she'd paddle.

Without any further explanation, Jake propelled them away from the ferry toward the shore.

He couldn't have just lowered them down with a rope? Beth's teeth chattered and the adrenaline that had flooded her body with the shock of cold continued to course through her bloodstream. Could hypothermia be in her future? She remembered the slightly frostbitten fingers she'd once witnessed from a fisherman who'd fallen overboard and shuddered. Chipped nail polish would be nothing compared with that! *Get a grip. You were in the water for twenty seconds max.*

Jake was there to protect her, and he'd had a good reason for everything else.

The kayak made good time, and they made it to shore quickly. Jake jumped out and dragged the vessel, with Beth still inside, onto land. He pulled off his life jacket and stowed it in the vacant seat. Extending his hand to Beth, he helped her out of the kayak and then her life jacket.

He gave her arms a firm rub. "I know it's cold, but we'll warm up when we walk." He grabbed the bags from the kayak and dug into one, pulling out a surprisingly dry jacket. "Here, replace your wet jacket with this."

Beth did as he said and instantly warmed up. "Where are we going?"

Jake slung the bags on his back and held out his hand. "Into town to find transportation."

"*Find* transportation? That's the plan?"

"Yes. I'm going to get you to Anchorage, don't worry."

Beth sighed, following through the scrubby evergreens. It had been longer than usual since she'd been to Valdez. She'd typically come every few weeks to see her friend Pamela... *Oh.* "I know someone who can help."

Thirty minutes later, they'd made it to the back of Café Valdez, and Beth was ready to collapse. Traipsing through the trees and scrub, then along residential streets to avoid the main roads, she wished Pamela and her husband, Craig, had located their café closer to the docks. Instead, they'd chosen a charming forest view, as far as possible from where the kayak had landed.

"Let's go in the back." Beth led Jake in behind the quaint, red-painted, wood building and up the steps. Pamela and Craig never locked the back door, so Beth went to open it before Jake stopped her.

"I need to check it first."

Beth waited for Jake to crack open the door, keeping her body between his and the wall. "Okay, it's clear."

They entered to sumptuous smells and chatter. The hall from the stairs led directly into the bustling café. Instead, Beth stepped into the dry storage area and pointed to the kitchen, where a kitchen hand washed dishes and a sous chef stirred a large pot of soup.

"Pamela will be in here somewhere. She's the chef." Beth poked her head around the door, and her friend's face lit up.

Wiping her hands on the tea towel tucked into a half-bistro apron, a brunette woman of short stature, in a light blue chef's jacket, climbed down from her double step-up stool and walked through the door to greet them. Beth bent down to give her a hug. Pamela was one of the only people to whom Beth had allowed herself to grow even a little bit close. Because she would never visit Beth in Cordova, and they primarily traded baked goods, Beth had hoped no one would notice. Besides, the woman wouldn't take no for an answer. She'd thawed Beth's defenses like sunbeams after a blizzard.

"It's great to see you, Beth, it's been ages!" Pamela took a couple of steps back and sized her up. "Only, there's something...different about you. What's up, hon?"

Beth caught her reflection in the shiny, stainless-steel, industrial fridge and gasped. *Oh no.* Her hair had lost its curl, lying in a damp, bedraggled mess. Lines of mascara smudged her cheeks, where the cuts had become tiny scabs. She hadn't considered it at the time, but the oversized jacket Jake had given her must be the ugliest shade of army green she'd even seen.

"It's a long story." What else could she say?

Jake stepped forward and held his hand down to Pamela, who took it. "Deputy US Marshal Jake Cruz. We have a bit of a situation. Do you have a car we can borrow for a day or two?"

He couldn't ask for *that*! Beth had expected to ask for maybe a cup of tea and some muffins, and the number of the local taxicab company. Not her friend's car.

Heat rose in her cheeks. "Forget he said that, Pam, it's too much to ask." Ignoring the black look Jake gave her, she continued. "A cup of tea would be lovely, though, if you have time."

Pamela's hands went to her hips. "Beth! Of course you can borrow my car. You'd do the same for me if I were in trouble." She pulled her keys from her pocket and handed them to Jake. "My car's the red Ford Focus out back." She gestured to her short stature. "As you might've guessed, it's been modified, but it drives exactly the same as a regular car. Just take out the cushions and mind the hand controls." She licked her lips. "As for that cup of tea, looks like you're in a rush. How about a couple of thermoses for the road, and some food to go?"

"Thanks, you're a good friend." Jake's words cut through Beth's embarrassment.

Beth's breath came a little easier. "If you're sure?"

Pamela waved the question away and returned to the kitchen, where she issued instructions to the sous chef then returned to them. "She'll be fine here for a few moments. Why don't you go sort out the car?" Jake looked between the two women and Pamela cocked an eyebrow. "You *looked* like you were in a hurry."

He gave Beth a hard stare. "Don't leave the kitchen."

Once Jake had left, Pamela yanked two stools over and gestured for Beth to sit. She hopped on the second one. "So, let's get this straight. You appear unannounced, looking like a drowned rat, with cuts all over your face, toting the most dangerous-looking US marshal I've ever seen? Spill!"

"I can't."

Pamela raised an eyebrow. "I'm lending you *my car.*"

The thought of anything happening to her friend made Beth's stomach clench. "You're right. I don't want any of this to come back to you, so just deny everything. Say we stole your car."

"What?" Her friend's eyes widened. "Go back a step. You know what you're talking about, but I have *no idea.*"

Beth blew out a breath. "Sorry, you're right. How do I even begin…" She swallowed. "I'm a witness for the FBI, and Deputy Cruz is protecting me. There are some people who I helped put into prison—trust me, you don't want to know more than that—and, well, things are a bit tricky at the moment." Understatement of the year.

"Tricky?" Pamela frowned, then she raised her hands to her mouth. "Car-bomb-level tricky?"

Beth swallowed. "You heard about that?"

"It's all anyone's talking about! If I'd known it was you..." Pamela blinked, pulled out her cell phone, and scrolled for a bit before showing Beth the news headline: Elementary School Bombing. A photo of the scene under the heading pictured a wide shot of the parking lot filled with emergency vehicles and the unrecognizable, smoldering remains of Beth's car.

"Oh no." Beth rubbed her forehead. "I shouldn't have come here. What was I thinking?"

"Nonsense. You're my friend, whether you're in danger or not." She reached for Beth's hand. "Although once you're out of this, I'm going to be calling in a favor."

Beth squeezed her hand. "Anything."

"Your peanut butter choc-chunk brownie recipe."

"Oh." Beth kept her recipes a closely guarded secret. "It's not written down, so you'll have to memorize it."

"I can do that."

Beth leaned forward. "Okay, so first you have to bloom half a cup of Dutch process cocoa in half a cup of boiling water for five minutes." She spoke in a low voice.

"No!" Pamela held up her hand. "Not *now*. Tell me when this is over. Even better, you can show me how you make them. I'm sure it's partly your technique." She tilted her head to the side. "Believe me, I've tried to replicate those little beauties."

Beth straightened and ran her hands through her knotty hair. "What if I don't come back?"

"You're coming back. The Lord isn't done with you yet, and neither am I."

The Lord? What did He care about Beth? She couldn't say that to Pamela. "I wish I had your faith."

Jake came through the door, wiping his hands on his pants. "You ready?"

"I'll check on that care package." Pamela hopped down from her stool and powered into the kitchen.

Beth turned to Jake. "I'm worried this is going to come back to Pamela, so I told her to say we stole her car. I hope that's okay?"

"Yeah, good idea. I've swapped out the number plates anyway."

"You what?" Beth took a step back. "How?"

Jake shrugged. "Another car in the parking lot. Why make it easy for them, huh?" He returned to the hallway, walked a little way toward the tables and craned his neck at the customers.

What about the poor people whose plates were stolen? Beth shuddered. How many innocent people would be harmed for her sake? How she wished she hadn't involved Pamela.

Her friend returned with a generous, fragrant package filled with food and drinks, and the lump in Beth's throat returned.

"My wallet's in my bag." Swallowing, she looked toward Jake, whose shoulders had stiffened.

Pamela smirked. "Your money's no good here, but…I wouldn't say no to your lemon curd recipe."

Beth reached down and embraced Pamela, tears welling in her eyes at the possibility of never seeing her friend again. "I'll throw in the coconut-mousse cookies too. And the key lime bars. I know you love those. Thank you so much."

Jake took two strides over to her, placed his hand on her shoulder and pulled her into the pantry. "We have company."

Pamela walked in with them. "'Company'?"

"The man who's after us just walked into your café."

Beth flinched. *Please don't let Pamela get hurt.*

FIVE

Pamela dusted off her hands. "I'll see to him myself."

Beth's stomach lurched, but before she could say a word, Jake placed his hand on Pamela's shoulder.

"Wait. Be strategic about it."

"Okay…" Pamela raised an eyebrow and winked at Beth.

She's not taking this very seriously! Beth's mind raced at the possibilities of what might befall her friend. Thankfully, Pamela had never had to deal with a Bulgarian criminal gang, but her lack of concern filled Beth with dread.

Jake pursed his lips, perhaps thinking the same thing. "Go serve him like you'd serve any customer. He'll probably ask if you've seen us. Tell him no, but you just started your shift, and you'll go check with your staff. Then come back out here. I'll dial the Valdez PD now, so hopefully that will be the end of it." Pamela rolled her shoulders and went to walk past them down the hall.

Jake stopped her. "Don't be a hero."

"Hero*ine*." Pamela gave him one of her signature pitiless looks.

"Heroine. Be careful." He held Beth back while Pamela left, then peered around the door before pulling her after him. "There's not much time. I'll stow you in the trunk until we're on the road."

The trunk? Beth's mouth fell open, white-hot terror coursing through her body. How her legs raced after him down the stairs, she had no idea, because inside she was frozen solid. "I'm claustrophobic."

The charcoal-colored trunk of Pamela's red Ford Focus yawned like the mouth of a catacomb.

Jake pressed his lips together. "I guess you can lie in the back seat." He reached for a blanket and shut the trunk.

Beth's shoulders relaxed and she climbed into the back, not complaining when Jake wrapped the blanket over her face. Moments later, Jake revved the engine, reversing out of the parking lot. Before they'd gone more than a few yards, he slammed on the brakes. "Wait here. Don't move."

Not waiting for an answer, Jake leaped from the car and slammed the door behind him.

What's happening? As tempted as Beth was to peek, she didn't want to risk it. Minutes passed. The blanket irritated her nose. Maybe she should take a look after all?

Bang! A deafening shot shattered the silence. *Pamela!* Her friend was inside. No way would she just lie here doing nothing. She peeled the blanket from her face and peeked through the window. The parking lot and street were clear. Something must be going on inside. Her heart pounded as she eased open the car door and crept toward the building. *Where's Jake?* Had *he* been shot? Sirens sounded in the distance.

She scaled the back stairs, peering through the kitchen window. No sign of Pamela or Jake. Before she could open the door, Jake flung it wide, rubbing his jaw as if he'd been hit.

When he saw her, his eyes clouded. "What part of *wait in the car* didn't you understand?"

"Is Pamela okay?" Beth's voice came out with a squeak.

The sirens grew closer and Jake grabbed her hand, pulling her back to the car. "She's fine."

"Phew!"

Jake gave a deep sigh and opened the front passenger door for her. "The man's been detained. You can ride shotgun."

"What happened?"

He slid behind the wheel and started the engine. "A local hunter shot the man when he pulled a gun and threatened Pamela. There was a scuffle, he's tied up and the police are almost here. Let's go while we still can."

Beth clipped her seat belt, and Jake pulled onto the highway, his head swiveling every which way. They weren't clear yet.

"You doing okay?" He glanced toward her then returned his eyes to the road, his fingers on the gold cross. "With the claustrophobia. I assume you left the car because I put a blanket on you."

Beth's breath hitched. He'd listened to what she'd said. "Um, yeah, I'm okay. When I'm not in a confined space, I'm fine. I was just worried about Pamela." *And you.* She licked her lips, suddenly thirsty. "Where's Pamela's care package?"

"Under your seat. You need me to reach it?"

"I've got it." Twisting in her seat, Beth waved her hand around until it connected with the bag. She pulled it out, retrieving a thermos from the side. "You want something? You must be starving by now."

"Sure, thanks."

Beth reached into the bag and pulled out a submarine sandwich. "Hmm, here you go. This is her most popular lunch item." She unwrapped the distinctive red paper slightly so he could eat with one hand. "Meatloaf sub. It's basically a meat*ball* sub, but without the risk of escaping meatballs."

Jake took a bite, then groaned. Beth had made such noises

before too—all involuntary, Pamela's food tasted *that* good. She popped the thermos lid and took a careful sip because the sous chef would've made it hot enough to last. Sure enough, the near-scalding tea needed to cool a little before it became drinkable. She pushed the thermos into the car door holder and grabbed a bottle of water. *Just what I needed.*

Jake had already eaten half the sub, but he stopped, handing it back to her. "I'll finish that later, unless you want it?"

"I'm good, thanks." She passed him the open bottle of water. "Here, wash it down with this."

He drank half the bottle then handed it back. "Thanks. That must be the best sub I've ever had. And I've had some great subs."

"Let's hope we live long enough to tell Pamela."

Jake took a longer glance this time. "The US Marshals Service has *never* lost a witness who followed our protocols. Ever. I'm not going to be the one to mess up that record, I promise you. Besides, with the caliber of assassins they've sent after us so far, we'll be in Anchorage in five hours. Right on schedule."

Beth gaped at him. The ego on the man! But to his credit, he'd kept her safe so far. Maybe her preference for Tom's protection was unwarranted. Time would tell. "I'm glad you're so confident."

A grunt was the only response. *Him and his grunts.* Beth pulled the bug out bag toward her and unzipped the compartment where her travel hairbrush and cosmetics were kept. Tom had suggested a waterproof bag, and everything remained dry. She set about detangling her hair, working through some dry shampoo and leave-in conditioner. The curl might be gone, but she could twist her locks into a style that might mask that.

"Why are you doing that?" Jake's question cut through the hum of the engine like a chainsaw.

"Pardon?"

"You don't need to fuss with your hair."

Beth frowned. "What do you mean? Of course I need to *fuss* with my hair. It's like a bird's nest."

"It's distracting." Jake's eyes flicked toward her then back to the road.

"Sorry. I'm almost done." She quickly twisted her hair into a low bun, securing the straggling locks with some bobby pins. Did he feel the same way about her makeup? Her panda eyes reflected in the window, and her fingers itched for her makeup bag. Pamela would have wet wipes in the glove compartment. Surely he couldn't object to that, at least. "I need to wipe my face, if that's okay?"

Jake grunted. Not a *no*.

She reached into the glove compartment, thankful for Pamela's predictability. Quickly wiping her face, her shoulders sank. Devoid of any makeup, she looked almost like her old self. Except with extra weight and green contacts. Those would have to come out soon, they were making her eyes itchy.

Half an hour later, clouds hovered over the Chugach Mountains as they climbed the pass. The evergreens lining the road had given way to low alpine scrub, which covered the moraine debris left by glaciers long gone. Yellow poles on the low side of the road marked the edge of the paved surface, an indication for the snowplows. The view out over the valley back toward Valdez, where one of the assassins remained in custody, reminded Beth of the reason she was there.

"The outcome of the appeal is today."

Jake cleared his throat. "Appeal?"

"Kamen Petrov, the gang leader. My testimony put him in

prison, but his lawyers found grounds to appeal. The judge is deciding today. Isn't that in the file?"

"There wasn't that level of detail about his appeal. How did you know?"

Beth licked her dry lips. "Tom set up an alert on my phone. Any time his name—or anyone who's involved in the case— is updated on the internet, I get a notification. His name appeared on the court list a couple of weeks ago."

"Do you think he'll win?"

A chill ran down Beth's spine. "It's unlikely. The facts are on the FBI's side. But I really hope he doesn't. If he does, there'll be a retrial and I'll have to testify again." And change her identity again, which looked more likely anyway. The thought made her heart sink.

Jake turned to her, eyebrows slightly raised. "You'd testify again? Even with everything that's happened?"

"I don't have a choice, do I? My safety won't change either way, but if I don't testify, he'll end up free and… I couldn't do that to his children."

"His children? What do you mean? You think Petrov would hurt his children?"

Beth's mind returned to the innocent faces of little Andrey and Dora. "No, it's not that. Well, not physically." She didn't want to get into the details. They appeared in her nightmares often enough.

"I don't understand. Was there something you saw that's not in the file?" Jake's sudden interest unnerved her. Plenty hadn't made it into the file. Why did he care? He wasn't in the FBI. His sole job was to deliver her safely to Anchorage.

"Don't worry about it. I'm just making conversation. There's nothing we can do now anyway."

Jake ran his hand over his shaved head before returning it to the steering wheel. "It's a long drive. Whatever's on your mind… I'm listening. Especially if you're worried about Petrov's children. You were their au pair. If anyone's opinion matters, it's yours."

The words came out with such unexpected gentleness, Beth's guard dropped a little. Maybe he did care. Seemed unlikely. But it wouldn't hurt to tell someone else. The FBI didn't seem particularly interested about the children, even when she'd tried to raise it. If something happened to her, maybe Jake could help them.

"The children are terrified of their father. He abuses their mother in front of them, and yells at them if they don't behave how he wants. Not like regular parent yelling. He becomes enraged, like it's uncontrolled. Scary. His standards are completely unrealistic, and I can only imagine how much happier their household must be with him behind bars."

Jake's jaw clenched. "The FBI didn't put that in the file."

"None of his behavior was technically reportable, or I would have reported it—I'm a mandated reporter. He's always been careful. Besides, the FBI were more concerned with getting Petrov convicted for the murders, which I can understand. I didn't push it because, if he stayed in prison, the problem would resolve itself. But if he returns to their home… I can't let that happen."

"I understand." His hands tightened around the steering wheel. "I won't let that happen either."

"What can *you* do?" The words left Beth's mouth before she could think.

Jake glanced at her with a slight grin. "Make it into a big deal."

Beth's heart warmed toward him. Finally, someone other than her and the children's mother seemed to care. "That sounds good to me."

"You were their au pair for two years?"

"Yeah. They're great kids. I often stayed overnight so their mom could take a sleeping pill. I think she'd become reliant on them to sleep. Only, one night…"

Jake gave her an understanding look. "You saw some things that you'll never forget."

A bitter tang entered her mouth. "I had my eyes opened to how appearances can be deceiving. People can put on charm and hospitality while all the while being evil."

Jake's gut churned at the thought of what he'd read. His words put Beth's experience mildly. Beth had been snoozing on the couch near Petrov's sitting room when Petrov had returned from dinner with six of his highest-ranking foot soldiers and some hangers on.

Petrov hadn't known about the arrangement between Beth and his wife, but it sounded like Beth had regularly stayed overnight then pretended to arrive the next morning. Mrs. Petrov must be a reasonable mother if she'd thought to have someone close by to look after the children if they woke in the night. In Jake's experience, many wouldn't bother. It said in the file that Mrs. Petrov hadn't mentioned Beth's sleeping overnight because she hadn't wanted to "upset" her husband. She'd made is sound like she was doing Beth a favor since she'd lived an hour away. From Beth's recent update, Jake mentally upgraded "upset" to mean Petrov would abuse his wife, and Beth had been the one doing the favor.

So, on the night that changed Beth's life, she couldn't reveal herself and make a quick exit. That would've come back on Mrs. Petrov. Instead, she'd hidden and overheard an extended conversation all about the organization's future. That they spoke in Bulgarian hadn't been a problem. Beth had been hired as au pair partly because of her impressive foreign language skills. A child of immigrants—her mother

Russian, her father Latvian—both languages were spoken at home, with English her third language. According to the file, she'd spent some of her college years studying linguistics in Eastern Europe where she learned several more, including Bulgarian, Petrov's native language. No denying she'd understood every word she'd heard that night, making her a valuable witness.

Unfortunately, the discussion had involved the dismissal of two disloyal foot soldiers, who were summarily executed. What made matters worse was that one of the replacements happened to be a US senator.

While the senator had not yet been charged with any crime, word was the FBI's case currently relied on Beth's critical eyewitness testimony. But at this stage, the focus was on Petrov. He was the man who stood to gain the most from Beth's death.

Jake could only imagine how frightening the experience must have been for Beth. Her courage, and care for the children, impressed him more than it probably should. She was a witness, not someone he should come to care about. Caring too much for a witness was always a mistake. So long as she kept those contact lenses in, everything should stay professional.

His phone rang and he checked it before answering. His boss.

"You got away safely?"

Jake had called his boss the moment the assailant at Pamela's café had been secured. They'd agreed that traveling to Anchorage by road presented the best option. "We're about half an hour south of Glennallen on the Richardson Highway. Our ETA to Anchorage is three and a half hours."

Forsyth harrumphed. "Do what you can to cut that in half. The FBI called. Petrov has won his appeal. Miss Ryder will have to give evidence again, and they're planning to stay on my back until she's in a safe house. I've assured them she's fine in your capable hands, so don't make me a liar." His boss's ambitious nature meant he demanded nothing but excellence from his team. Not that Jake had a problem with excellence, but there were ways of motivating a team that worked better than others. Micromanagement wasn't one of them.

Jake's stomach hardened, and he glanced at Beth, whose face was set in a grim line. She'd obviously heard every word—no surprise given Forsyth's unsubtle, booming voice. "Yes, sir." He ended the call.

"He won his appeal." The resignation in her voice quickly turned to anger. "How could the prosecutor let that happen? Now I have to change my identity again, and it won't be in Cordova, that's for sure." She sighed. "I like Cordova. I guess I could dye my hair black next time. What do you think? Brown eyes? Maybe I should get some surgery too. I've never liked my nose, and I could probably do with higher cheekbones."

Brown contacts would be a complete travesty, but the thought of her surgically altering her appearance made his gut churn. "There's nothing wrong with your nose. Or any other part of you." He'd said it out loud without meaning to.

She stared at him, her mouth slightly parted. "Really?"

Jake shrugged, swallowed and scowled; glad he didn't have Beth's habit of blushing at the slightest embarrassment. He should *not* be thinking about her nose, her cheeks or any other part of her. But she'd earned at least a crumb of support. "I'll deny I said this, but you're right about the prosecutor. They've had plenty of time to prepare for the appeal. They've probably spent most of their resources on the case against Senator Bakalov."

Beth's shoulders drooped. "I sure hope so. I still can't believe they let him continue sitting in the senate."

"As far as the general public is concerned, he's squeaky clean. He hasn't even been charged, and any association with Petrov didn't come out at trial for fear of contaminating the case against him. The FBI only get one shot, and the stakes are even higher than the Petrov case." *Let's hope they get it right this time. Lord, we sure could use Your justice.*

"You're right. I'm just grumbling." She let out a long, slow breath.

Jake softened. Beth didn't deserve any of this, let alone his judgment. "You have every right to grumble." He pursed his lips. Should he apologize for complaining about her primping? No, that was a bridge too far. She looked better without makeup anyway. *Not that that has anything to do with anything.* Time to change the subject. "I wouldn't say no to the rest of that sub."

Beth rustled around until she found the sandwich, unwrapped it, then handed it to him. Even lukewarm, the flavor was spectacular. She reached into the bag and pulled out a sandwich for herself, quietly munching as they drove on.

They'd been driving for another hour or so, and the sun beamed through the windshield on its long, slow passage toward the west. The scenery had changed, with soft tundra and thick, low brush broken up by drifts of evergreen trees. A dark silver Toyota Tacoma appeared in Jake's rearview mirror, gaining on them. Since his boss's stern missive, Jake had been traveling a good fifteen miles over the sixty-five mile per hour speed limit, so the truck must be traveling at about ninety. No coincidence, as far as Jake's gut was concerned. *Where are all these bad guys coming from?*

"There's someone tailing us." He pressed the accelerator

to the floor, and the little car gave a sluggish leap forward. Pamela's lax car servicing history was becoming apparent.

Beth immediately turned to look. "How can you be sure?"

"Experience. They're probably going to try and run us off the road, so I need you to secure any projectiles and brace for impact."

She immediately obeyed, stuffing her thermos into the glove compartment and wedging the bag under her seat. "Can't you outrun them?"

Jake grunted, choosing not to insult Pamela's car. Even if it'd had a full-service record, the lightweight hatchback wasn't a Ferrari. He also didn't want to trust too much in the little car's ability to hug the road. The twists and turns were almost as inconvenient as the frost heaves that created dips and peaks in the road. Whoever trailed them would have to deal with the same issues, albeit with a purpose-built vehicle.

"What happens when they catch us?" The fear in Beth's voice cut through him. He didn't like the feeling.

He dialed his boss and prayed he'd managed to secure some backup. Like Jake, Forsyth's home office was in Chicago, so he might be at a disadvantage in Anchorage when it came to resources.

"We have company, sir. Can you send anyone to help?"

"I'll do my best. Most of the marshals are at the wharf dealing with the fallout from a large asset seizure. I've called in reinforcements, but they may not be here for some time. Everyone's stretched thin." His boss's voice broke up a little. Must be going through an area with patchy coverage.

The Tacoma had gained on them further, even with Jake's sharp acceleration. The grille loomed in the rearview mirror, maybe ten yards behind. They'd end up off the road, even into the river, if he wasn't careful.

"There must be some Alaska State Troopers nearby. Highway patrol? Boy Scouts? I'll take anyone." He didn't voice his thoughts—no point increasing Beth's already high fear levels—but he trusted the joke would stress the urgency of the situation.

His supervisor let out a long breath. "I have your location. I'll send whoever I can."

They'd better make it quick; his phone was almost out of battery.

Jake ended the call and took his foot off the accelerator. The truck swung out beside them. A slight bend in the road shifted the balance, and as Jake slammed on the brakes, the truck nudged into them, sending them spinning onto the shoulder.

His mind returned to an uncomfortable thought that had plagued him since the ferry. *How do they keep finding us?*

SIX

Jake recovered the car from its spin and accelerated away from the Tacoma down a narrow, winding, unpaved road. Wherever it led, they were committed, with no way back to the Glenn Highway. To her credit, Beth hadn't made a sound. She'd simply braced her body against the seat, her right hand gripping the armrest for dear life. Navigating the hairpin bends and potholes became difficult at this speed, and the Ford bumped and slid, scraping against the foliage.

They bounced up onto the bridge and the Tacoma revved behind them. *Lord, please don't let us end up in the river.* Safely across, Jake navigated another hairpin bend, praying no one would be coming the other way. Where were they heading?

A sign came into view—Matanuska Glacier Tours—and Jake's heart sank. He'd brought them on a one-way journey to nowhere.

Movement in the rearview mirror caught his attention. The Tacoma was gaining on them. Jake floored it. Then, *bang, bang, bang*! Bullets pinged off the back of Pamela's car. Beth gasped.

"Get down!" Jake temporarily took a hand from the wheel to press Beth's shoulders below the windows. He'd have to take his chances and pray that God remained on his side today. He touched the cross around his neck and accelerated into a bend. The tires protested and spun on the muddy gravel before they caught, lurching ahead.

The silty, glacial river surged beside them. How far were they from the highway? One? Two miles? The bends were disorienting, and Pamela's odometer wasn't easy to see with the extra hand attachments she needed. Streaks of sunlight pierced the clouds and illuminated the blue of the glacier, reflecting the late-afternoon light. The Chugach Mountains rose behind it. There was no cover, and the road looked about ready to run out. No chance of getting away clean. The Tacoma rammed their bumper, buffeting their car toward the river. Jake corrected course, swerving into what appeared to be a parking lot. He zigzagged, the Tacoma on his tail, and zoomed down the last of the gravel road. They were hemmed in.

"We'll run out of bullets before they do. Get ready to make a break for it."

Beth's mouth gaped. "Where? There's nowhere to go!"

"Backup will come before long, don't worry." More of a hope than a certainty, but sometimes hope could be enough to keep a protected witness from breaking down. And he needed Beth as calm as possible.

The car juddered and slid toward the glacier, ending its service in an icy puddle.

"Brace!" Jake yelled.

They flexed for impact as the Tacoma ploughed into the rear, propelling the Ford Focus along the slippery flat and onto the muddy edge of the glacial river. Wind whipped the surface, and clouds covered the sun.

He glanced over his shoulder, drawing a deep, tactical breath. The Tacoma had braked after impact and remained twenty feet back. The airbags had deployed, impairing their view of him and Beth. That gave a few moments before the men would be upon them. "Let's go." He pulled on his backpack, drew his weapon, threw open the door and dragged Beth behind him. Crouching near the wheel, he used two precious bullets to shoot out the Tacoma's windscreen. A small distraction. Might buy them another few seconds. Then he pulled Beth after him toward the glacier. She ran surprisingly fast, gasping as she went. Not as fast as he'd prefer, but at a good enough pace to gain valuable space between them and the bullets. Whether adrenaline or Beth's fitness did the heavy lifting, Jake didn't care. As long as it continued for at least another few hundred yards. By then they'd be upon the outcrop of sediment and boulders that would offer some cover.

He glanced back again. One man alighted from the vehicle and took aim with his handgun. Where was the other one? Had he shot him? How many were there? He jerked Beth to the side and a couple of bullets flew past them. The man lowered his pistol and reached into the back, drawing out a hunting rifle. Another man climbed from the truck, a cell phone to his ear. Must be calling in reinforcements. Their time was running out. The OCG seemed to have more resources than the USMS, even if they weren't as highly skilled. He could do with an Alaska State Trooper right about now, or even a member of the local army ROTC.

Jake didn't know the terrain well, but he knew enough about the area to understand they must try to skirt the glacier without climbing onto its surface. Deprived of ice cleats and helmets, and with darkness hours away, they could suffer broken limbs—or worse, if they ended up on the glacier itself. They were thirty yards from cover when the crack of the rifle echoed off the glacier. Beth gasped when a bullet imbedded itself a foot from her ankle. Too close.

"Come on." Jake pushed Beth in front of him, hoping his backpack would slow any bullet that landed, if they didn't make it in time.

Another crack, and the bullet grazed Jake's jacket. The next would go right through them. He yanked Beth to the ground and the next bullet sailed over their heads. Only a few yards to cover, but what then? They couldn't stay there. The men would be after them, and the reinforcements would be on top of them.

He pulled Beth behind the boulders and let her rest. She panted, her breath ragged. Sweat beaded on her brow. He checked his phone. No reception. Two percent battery. Great. Pulling binoculars from the backpack, he surveyed their surrounds. The men were packing up, preparing to come after them. They seemed well prepared with crampons, heavy coats, gloves, even head lamps. Did they think they'd be out here when it grew dark? He had no intention of that happening. Between them they carried the Marlin bolt-action hunting rifle, a couple of pistols each and what looked like a Colt AR-15 semiautomatic rifle. If he didn't know different, he'd think they were overprepared for a hunting expedition. His gut dropped—in a sense they were. He and Beth had maybe two minutes' head start. The only way they could get some distance between the men and them, without being sitting ducks, was to use the boulders as cover. And that meant heading straight for the glacier. Jake's jaw clenched. The opposite of what he wanted.

"Stay low and close. We need to move quickly and quietly." Easier said than done with the loose stones and sediment they'd have to traverse.

Beth clambered to her feet and bent over, her head low. Jake pushed her in front of him, glancing back every so often to check that the men weren't visible. It was a risky move—

while the men couldn't see them, he couldn't see the men either. How fast he and Beth moved would be the difference between survival and death. Couldn't be helped. They were in God's hands now.

Beth's legs ached and pain stabbed her lungs with every breath. Jake's guiding palm on her back was the only thing that kept her going. That and the fear of catching a bullet. How had things come to this? They should be in Anchorage, or at least most of the way there. And what about Pamela's car? Smashed, possibly beyond repair, with at least one bullet hole! Beth's entire catalog of recipes could not repay that kind of damage.

Her foot caught on a stone and her ankle rolled painfully to the side. *Not now!* A sprained ankle could be the end of them. Somehow, Jake caught her before she'd caused herself any damage and moved her in the right direction with a gentle shove. The moonscape of glacial silt and sediment stretched ahead, and she avoided the puddles and ice patches in her way.

Jake pulled her to the ground with unexpected suddenness. A bullet whistled past them, followed by another.

"Run for the glacier, I'll cover you." He stood like a human shield and returned fire.

Beth ran, propelled by sheer terror. She stumbled and slipped, righting herself. The ground became silt-covered ice. She'd made it to the glacier. Now what?

A bullet slammed into the ice beside her, and she hit the ground. Jake's feet pounded toward her, and she turned to see a look of deep concern on his face.

"They missed," she gasped. "I'm okay."

More bullets followed, somehow missing them. Jake grabbed her by the upper arm and dragged her to her feet, turning to fire. A yell of pain from one of the men suggested Jake had hit his mark. *Will backup come?* What would they do if Jake ran out of bullets? Throw icicles?

If she turned her ankle again, that wouldn't matter. She concentrated on the terrain in front of her, where the slipperiness of the glacier was surpassed only by the treacherous obstacles—little rivers, rocks and dimples in the ice threatened to spill her back down the slope. At least she'd listened to Tom's advice and worn sturdy hiking boots. He'd drilled that into her when he'd educated her on the benefits of the bug out bag. Navigating a glacier in Mary Janes or kitten heels would've been deadly. Remembering Tom's absence at this moment didn't fill her with trepidation like it had earlier. Jake had proven himself competent enough, getting them out of some dangerous situations. Would he manage to get them out of this one?

They made it over the ridge only to find a sign had been posted not to proceed past the point. Jake ignored it, dragging her with him down the slope. They continued on and Beth's heart hammered against her ribs. There was always a good reason to post a sign like that. What awaited them? Blue ice peaks tore at the sky like jagged fingers, and Beth's breath caught. Would this be her first and last experience of touching a glacier? She'd taught her class about glaciers during the winter term—they'd made a big, messy model using salt dough, papier-mâché and lots of poster paint—and she knew a handful of facts about this one. The Matanuska Glacier stretched twenty-seven miles long and four miles wide. It began between the mountains and terminated at the mouth of the Matanuska River. While it might be the only glacier accessible by car in the country, that accessibility dwelled at one end only. And they were running in the opposite direction.

Jake's hand in hers brought her some comfort. At least he appeared to know what he was doing. She staggered on, stumbling and tripping as they went. Soon the men would be upon them again, and what then? Did Jake plan for them to go across the glacier and double back? Surely more men would be waiting for them when they returned. Maybe some friendlies, too, if Jake's boss came through. What she wouldn't give to see Officer Miller and Officer O'Halloran right about now. But they would be back in Cordova with their families.

They climbed a ramplike section, and Beth held her breath. Wouldn't this elevation expose them to the men and their guns? Reaching the crest, she risked a glance back and saw only ice. Jake had navigated them behind the jagged shards she'd spotted earlier. Her breath came out in visible puffs now, and the smell of ozone and frost burned her nose.

The ice dropped away to form a glacial lake, reminding her of how long it had been since her last drink of water. Though she'd love the chance to stop, rest and quench her thirst, they continued, skirting away from the lake and into the icy mounds.

Beth had no sense of their location on the glacier, but she knew how long they'd been out there. The sun's position meant they were heading toward five o'clock. They had little more than five hours of light ahead of them, and the time elapsed on the glacier didn't fill her with optimism.

Her legs grew heavy, her feet frozen. Stepping over an ice ridge, her foot slipped and she stamped heavily to the side. Instead of stopping her fall, the crust gave way. Both legs slipped through and she plunged into a crevasse with a shriek. Jake dropped to the ground in time to grab her wrist and stop her fall, but her body had already descended below the surface.

"Are you hurt?" He breathed heavily, his voice a hushed whisper.

"No." The scrapes and muscle pain didn't count. Besides, he'd saved her from tumbling further into the crevasse. How had he managed to grab her before she'd slipped to her death?

Jake changed his grip, but it didn't alter the ache in her wrist where he held her. Her legs flailed in the void, and he attempted to haul her out. Resistance hindered them both. She'd become wedged somehow, her hips caught at an odd angle. Wriggling and twisting, she tried to free herself but couldn't gain any traction.

"I think I'm stuck."

He tugged again, and tears pricked her eyes. Her arm felt like it could be wrenched from its socket at any moment. Jake grunted, then changed his prone position and peered down the crevasse, his other hand now gripping her arm too. "I'm going to lower you down."

Beth's stomach lurched. "What!"

"It's not far."

Before she could protest, he pushed her shoulder through the crevasse and lowered her until she dangled a foot or so above the base of the glacier. "What if the ice is thin? What if I fall straight through?" Her voice came out in a startling squeak.

Another grunt. "Try and stick the landing." He let go.

Her feet hit the ice with a crunch and the breath she didn't know she'd been holding whooshed out of her as she staggered against the wall. Before she could think, Jake's backpack landed beside her, shortly followed by him.

"What if we get trapped? What if there's no way out?" The icy walls began to close in on her and she stifled a scream.

He set his jaw and ignored the question, then grasped her hand and pulled her behind him along the crevasse. The ice cracked and hissed beside her, and the sound of running water sent shivers down her spine. Shadowed dimples pocked the ice walls, with hues of white, steel and ice-blue. The smooth floor must have been carved out by trickling underground streams. If it rained… She'd heard stories of people who'd frozen to death in crevasses, although they were much deeper. What if this one got deeper? What if they fell through the bottom? The crevasse narrowed and the sky became a sliver. Her breathing accelerated and her insides churned with anxiety. A whimper escaped, and Jake glanced back and gave her hand a squeeze.

"We'll be out of here soon. I've got you. Try not to make a sound." His low voice reminded her of the threat that loomed as large as the glacier. If the men heard her, they were sunk, trapped with nowhere to go.

They slowly crunched their way along the base of the crevasse, and Beth lost track of time. The claustrophobic space had closed over them completely, and they appeared to be walking through the world's skinniest cathedral, with icicles hanging like daggers above her head.

Jake must've pulled a small flashlight from somewhere, because now an eerie glow lit the space. *Does this mean we're going deeper into the ice?* She'd become disoriented early on, relying on Jake's sense of direction. An involuntary shudder rippled down her spine and she couldn't stop the tears. Would they die in this icy crypt? No one would ever find their bodies. At least her tears temporarily warmed her freezing cheeks. The cold of the crevasse seeped through her body, chilling her skin. The scrape of their shoes against the ice masked her sniffles—at least, she hoped they did. How humiliating to blubber when she'd kept it together so far.

Just as she thought her fate had been sealed, Jake stopped, snapping off the light. Shafts of natural light illuminated their surrounds once more. He turned and held his finger to his lips, then crept toward the light. Voices. Were the men lying in wait? Had they walked into a trap?

SEVEN

Beth's breath hitched when Jake let go of her hand and motioned for her to remain in place. How was she supposed to stay calm in the crevasse without even a friendly hand to hold? She stepped toward him, and he held out his hand again, giving her a stern look and slowly mouthing, *Wait here*. He pulled out his gun and edged toward the opening, his back against the wall. When he disappeared from sight, Beth's gut flipped. What if he didn't make it back? She closed her eyes, trying to imagine something pleasant, but her mind went blank. *What's taking him so long?*

When she'd become past ready to creep toward the opening, he reappeared and gestured for her to come. Beth's heart leaped, and she raced toward him like he'd sounded a starter's pistol. Finally, out of the crevasse! Ahead of her stood three people who seemed about her age—two men and a woman—and who regarded her with curiosity and suspicion. They wore life jackets, helmets and wet-weather gear. Were they tourists? Why were they out on the glacier at this time of the day?

Not that they were far on the glacier. Beth realized the river lay no more than a few yards behind them. She glanced back at the crevasse. The towering ice of the glacier posed the only threat. Where had the men gone?

Jake leaned into Beth. "They're tour guides. They were paddling along the river and saw our car. Thought we might be in trouble."

The woman stepped forward, a cell phone to her ear. "Are you injured? I'm on the phone with a 9-1-1 dispatcher."

"I'm fine." Beth startled when Jake's hand took hers. What had he told them? The tour guides needed to get out of here, or Petrov's men might shoot them too.

"We need to leave, now. Is there a back way out? We can't return to the parking lot." He spoke quietly.

Beth wanted to question him but bit her tongue. He was the expert here, not her. Surely, he didn't want the tour guides to be hurt any more than she did.

"The only way out *is* by the parking lot." Confusion filled the woman's face.

One of the men stepped forward, his jaw set. Since dealing with the FBI, Beth had learned to assess people, and he had a look about him that suggested a little less innocence than the others. Perhaps he was a veteran. "I can paddle you out."

Jake's brow furrowed. "To where?"

"Not far at this time of the day, but there are plenty of access points. Might be risky to go down the rapids—"

"I'll take my chances." Jake used that tone he'd used with the principal, Mrs. Sutton.

The man shrugged, as if to say, *Your funeral.* "Follow me."

"Help is on the way." The woman ended her call.

"You two head back, I'll take the deputy to the river." They handed their life jackets to Jake and Beth, then dithered. "Carrie, Daniel, go. Be careful."

The other man and woman nodded, hustling away from them, their cleats biting into the ice.

"I'm Ethan Harris, formerly Third Marine Raider Battalion."

Like Tom. Beth allowed herself to relax a little.

"You're a water native, then. Appreciate your help." Jake didn't make further introductions, and Ethan didn't appear offended.

Ethan set a fast pace, and Jake let Beth go first, following behind. They skirted alongside the river, the remaining silt-covered ice making the journey longer than it might've if she and Jake had the right shoes. Ethan didn't seem concerned by their slow progress, but his gun remained out of its holster. "I take it you're WITSEC? Who are we up against?"

"Bulgarian assassins." Jake's voice remained low, and Beth sensed an edge to it. Did he know something she didn't?

They soon cleared the glacier from the opposite side to where they'd entered. The parking lot was nowhere in sight, but two kayaks—a tandem and a single—had been moored on the shore.

Ethan gestured to the two-man kayak. "I'll paddle you down to Hicks Creek. That'll get you out of immediate danger, and you can regroup. No rapids necessary."

"Thanks. Do you have a phone I can use? Mine's dead."

"Sure." Ethan unlocked his phone and handed it to Jake, who dialed.

"It's me, sir. Any news on those deputies?"

While Jake updated his boss, letting him know their location and plans, Ethan pushed the tandem kayak out to the edge of the river, ready for launch, and helped Beth into the front seat. He checked the straps on her life jacket and handed her a paddle. "I'm sure you have a story to tell."

Beth wasn't sure how to answer the question, so she shrugged. "I'm sure you have a few as well."

Ethan grinned. "Maybe next time." He seemed about to say something more when Jake strode toward them, scowling. Ethan accepted his phone back and launched his kayak.

Jake propelled them into the river and followed Ethan, who'd already paddled twenty feet ahead. Did he get bad news from his boss? Hopefully, he'd fill her in soon. The not knowing made Beth's stomach heavy.

Beth glanced behind her to check on him, and her heart froze. On top of the glacier, the silhouette of man stood, rifle raised. "Jake!"

Jake turned then called out to Ethan. "Duck!" He shoved Beth forward.

Ethan didn't hesitate, ducking before the first bullet flew over them. He turned, surprisingly calm, squinting toward the man on the glacier. "What is that, a Marlin? He's not a great shot, is he?"

"He doesn't have to be if he spends enough bullets." Jake had already begun paddling frantically. "We need another hundred yards and he'll be out of range. Beth, stay down."

Jake and Ethan paddled quickly, weaving to and fro, avoiding the bullets until they paddled out of range and the shots passed harmlessly into the water behind them.

"Will your friends be okay?" Jake pulled up alongside Ethan's kayak.

"I'll warn them." Ethan pressed a wireless earpiece into his ear and kept paddling. The rushing river rendered his words unintelligible.

They paddled without speaking for half an hour or so, Jake doing most of the work. Aside from an American kestrel that hovered over the bank of the river before dropping toward its prey, Beth barely noticed any wildlife. Thankfully, the flow of the river stayed fairly smooth and her seasickness didn't return.

Ethan slowed his kayak and pulled up beside Jake and Beth, indicating ahead to a pebbled inlet with his paddle. "This is where I'm landing. I've got to pack up the kayaks, then I'll be heading home to Sutton once I've checked in with Carrie and Daniel, if you want a ride in that direction?"

"Thanks, that'd be great." Jake followed Ethan, paddling the kayak up onto the bank, then climbing out to help Beth. She stumbled a little, not realizing her legs had turned numb. Jake caught her, holding her to his chest while she found her feet. "You okay?"

Goose bumps traveled up her arms. "Yeah, thanks."

He pulled away and picked up the kayak, following Ethan. They hadn't gone ten feet before the dark silver Tacoma fishtailed down the driveway toward them. Jake dropped the kayak, reached for his pistol and pressed Beth behind him. "Stay down."

To her surprise, Ethan did the same. Why was a tour guide armed?

"Go back to the river!" Ethan yelled the instructions over his shoulder and backed toward them. "I'll cover you."

The two men jumped from the vehicle and fired.

Ethan returned fire, hitting one of the men square in the chest. The man stumbled backward against the door of the truck, breathing heavily. The other man ducked behind the side of the truck.

Jake hesitated. "They've got body armor, and you're outgunned. I'm not leaving you here alone."

"I've got this. Carrie called the troopers, they'll be here soon. I have a rifle and more ammo in my Jeep. Cover me, then go." He ran across the open area, and Jake shot at the men until Ethan had made it safely behind a clapped-out Jeep Wrangler.

Grabbing Beth and the kayak, Jake ran to the shallow bank, pushed her in front and launched them onto the river. Shots rang out after them, and Beth hoped Ethan would have enough ammunition.

"You need to paddle too." Jake's voice rasped behind her, and she dipped her paddle into the water, attempting to mimic the strokes she'd seen Ethan perform. "Good. Keep going."

Beth wanted to ask if he knew where they were headed, but that would have to wait. Instead, she concentrated on her paddling, and her arms soon burned from the effort. The rush of water masked any other sounds, and the river ran under a bridge, sending Beth's heart into palpitations. Hopefully, Ethan and the Alaska State Troopers could take care of the men. If they didn't, it would be easy for them to shoot at the kayak from the road or a bridge. She and Jake wouldn't hear them until it was too late. *Don't think about it.*

Ahead, the rushing grew louder, and the silty, gray-brown water frothed white. Sheer rock walls towered above them on one side, confining the river and their options. Evergreens flanked the other side, and rocks rose to meet them in the river. Beth's stomach lurched and nausea threatened. Surely seasickness was confined to the sea. She stifled a shriek when the rapids buffeted the kayak and turned it around. They were traveling backward, the kayak pitching like a roller coaster. Dizzy, and feeling a little green around the gills, she gripped the paddle, terrified she might let go. Jake righted them and maneuvered the hull around a large boulder that jutted out of the middle of the river.

He yelled over the clamor of the water. "If you fall in, point your feet downstream. You don't want your back or your head to hit a rock."

Beth's stomach contracted. *Fall in?* Her eyes widened and she fought to retain control of her emotions as much as her stomach. She had a life jacket. The life jacket would keep her afloat. Legs forward, feet in front. She could do that, couldn't she? *Don't fall in.* That must be the better option.

The kayak rolled and shook, and bile rose in her throat. At least if she disgraced herself now, the river would wash it away. Jake had already seen her at her worst. Glacial water sloshed over the hull and drenched her torso. She wiped the wet tendrils of hair away from her eyes and concentrated on not falling in. How she wished they were on dry land. The kayak pitched and fell as the water level dropped through a rapid. Her stomach lurched and she gave in, hanging her head over the side.

"Are you okay?" Jake had to raise his voice to be heard.

Beth shook her head. No point pretending.

"Hang in there, you're doing great. Try to stay loose in the hips and roll with the swells."

Doing great? She sure didn't feel like it.

"I'll find a safe place before dark, okay?"

Having given up any pretense of helping with the paddling, Beth's shoulders slumped. The highway followed the river. How on earth could he find a safe place? The kayak continued to buck and roll, and moments later, it scraped over a submerged rock and capsized. Beth didn't realize the danger until she hung upside down in the water, disoriented and pinned by the kayak.

Help!

I can't have lost her. Jake's heart pounded. He scrabbled around in the swirling glacial silt, trying to catch hold of Beth. That rock had come out of nowhere. If he'd been up front, he might have seen it, but maybe not. He'd easily disengaged from the kayak, muscle memory from the kayaking adventures of his youth kicking in. He seized the grab handle to stop himself from floating away. Why wasn't the kayak moving? And where'd Beth gone? Her life jacket should have rebounded her to the surface too. Unless she'd become pinned under the kayak.

He inhaled a deep breath and plunged into the water, grasping the grab handle for support. Fighting against the life jacket's buoyancy, his hands connected with her hair. He fumbled around until his fingers found the top of her life vest. Giving it a yank downward, he dislodged her from the cockpit, then hooked his arms under her shoulders and pulled. Her body remained limp, and adrenaline fizzed through him. *Lord, You've kept her safe so far, please help me now.* Jake's lungs burned and he brought her to the surface, attempting to catch the side of the kayak. He missed. Freed of its cargo, the kayak bobbed away down the river, and the current dragged him to the middle. Beth's head lolled to the side. He had to get her out. The slightly alkaline, salty tang of glacial silt coated his tongue; he prayed it wasn't impeding Beth's airways.

A dogleg in the river approached, and Jake kicked for the bank with all his strength. Snagging his arm on the large pebbles, he levered them toward the bank, propelling Beth onto dry ground before joining her. He turned her on her side and gave her a whack between her shoulder blades. She coughed up a mouthful of milky-brown water. Jake's eyes turned heavenward. *Thank You, Lord.* He rubbed Beth's back, and she coughed up a little more and groaned. Pulling her upright, he held her to him and wiped the hair out of her eyes. Her head turned to rest under his chin, and he allowed himself to relax. The highway wasn't close by on this stretch of river, thankfully. It would make it harder for anyone to find them—friend or foe. But that didn't matter at present. *Thought I'd lost you for a moment.*

Beth licked her lips, coughed and swallowed, murmuring, "Are we there yet?"

The ridiculousness of her words tickled him, and Jake chuckled, his whole body shaking as much from the cold and the adrenaline as the laughter. "We're somewhere, that's for sure. Let's get you dry."

He clambered to his feet, pulling Beth up with him. She'd probably prefer to rest, but too bad. They needed to keep moving or risk hypothermia. They'd landed on the wrong side of the river, the south side, and the temperature had dropped. With the highway on the north side, no one could get to them here, which had advantages and disadvantages. On the plus side, the forest offered them plenty of cover. He'd have to make a fire, then he could work out their next steps.

An hour later, the sun had dipped behind the mountains and Jake had started a fire. Beth's outer clothes were strung next to the heat, and her thermals were hopefully drying on her as she sat, wrapped in a space blanket. The physical activity of collecting wood and setting Beth up near the fire had helped to keep him warm, but as he paused near the flames, an icy breeze chilled his back. The smell of birch smoke reminded him of Fairbanks, where he and his siblings had toasted marshmallows. Deployed all over the place, he barely saw them anymore. Photos and updates on the family messaging group kept them in touch. Not that he'd be updating them on this.

Wolves howled nearby, and Jake's muscles tensed. A hungry pack of wolves usually wasn't a threat to humans, but that depended on whether tourists had been feeding them. Their peak hunting times were dawn and dusk, and the pack might happily track him and Beth into the night if they considered humans a source of food. The fire would protect them—until it died down. But without any equipment, camping wasn't an option. They'd have to walk on through the night. He glanced at Beth, noticing with ambivalence that her contact lenses were gone. Her hair had dried in loose strands, her eyes in the firelight now the blue of the crevasse they'd escaped. Perhaps sensing him watching her, she returned his gaze. He should look away, but he couldn't.

"Do you wish you'd eaten some of my brownies while you had a chance?"

Jake raised an eyebrow, though he smiled inside. She must be feeling better if she was thinking about food. "Chocolate gives me migraines."

Her mouth gaped. "*All* chocolate?"

"White chocolate is fine."

"Huh. So, what is it about non-white chocolate that's a problem?"

Jake moved closer to the fire, warming his hands. "The brown part."

Beth laughed. "Sounds scientific. You know, I make cranberry and *white* chocolate cookies at Christmastime." She shivered. "If we make it to Christmas, I'll send you a batch. Wherever it is you live."

"Chicago. Like you." Where her case was based, and where she'd have to return to give evidence.

"*Not* like me. Cordova's my home now."

The answer surprised him. "Villani said you missed Chicago."

She pressed her lips together. "I did, but Cordova's grown on me. I just miss my mom."

Jake's heart softened. "Hopefully, you'll see her soon."

"Yeah." Beth's face dropped, like she didn't believe him.

"You'll be back in Chicago before you know it." Even to him, Jake's words sounded flat. Much depended on the prosecutor and the justice system, and after that appeal…

Beth stood. "I'm sure you're right. I mean, you've done a good job so far. Even if Tom would've… Never mind." She stopped herself, reaching for her jacket, which appeared dry. "Are we going to keep moving? I'd rather not be dinner for those wolves."

Jake's lips parted and his heart rate increased. He guessed she was about to say, *Even if Tom would've done a better job*. Things suddenly made sense. Beth must've imprinted onto Villani like a gosling onto the first mother figure it saw. Did he have it in him to earn that kind of trust? His mind returned to the words his fiancée had spoken the day she'd smashed the entire future he'd planned out for them. *You're just not good enough*. The remembered pain stabbed at him like an ice pick. His fiancée had also told him he'd paid more attention to his witnesses than to her. He'd hold on to that. Maybe he wasn't good enough to earn Beth's respect, but he could keep her safe.

Pulling her pants, blouse and jacket over her thermals, she wound her hair into a bun, not even bothering with a finger comb. She folded the space blanket and tucked it into the backpack. So much for his opinion of her high-maintenance nature.

He pulled the backpack onto his back. "Let's go." He grabbed the three-foot green branch he'd prepared earlier with black spruce pinecones and sap as a torch. He'd light it if wolves grew close, otherwise they could walk by whatever light the moon might provide. No point drawing attention to themselves.

They returned to the river and walked along the narrow path that the animals must use, heading toward Palmer. Once they reached the town, Jake planned to track down the local PD and get help. The cloud cover had dissipated, allowing the stars and moon to light their way. The track narrowed and they were surrounded by dense scrub. Rushing water masked Beth's steps behind him, and he wondered if he should let her go first.

No sooner had he dismissed the thought than a scrawny-looking, juvenile wolf appeared on the path ahead. Had this wolf been following them, or had they wandered into its territory? Usually lone wolves would avoid people, but this one looked hungry. Maybe it had been kicked out of its pack. The animal's tail rose and its ears stuck straight up. Teeth bared, its snout wrinkled. Such a threatening stance did not bode well.

Jake reached behind him and pulled Beth against his back. "Don't move."

EIGHT

Jake's heart picked up at the sight of the wolf. Predatory attacks were vanishingly rare, but higher than zero. Fortunately, like bears, they were susceptible to being hazed. A flaming torch would ward it off. He reached for the matches he'd stowed in his pocket. Drawing them out, he struck one, but it didn't light. He tried again. Nothing. Had they become too damp to catch? He'd wrapped them in plastic. Maybe the humidity from the river had done some damage.

The wolf growled. Jake considered his pistol, then discounted the idea. There had to be a way out without shooting this wolf. He had invaded the wolf's space, not the other way around. Besides, a gunshot would attract attention. Then he remembered his penlight. Wolves had excellent night vision, so disrupting that might be painful, much like turning on the light when someone wore night vision goggles. Maybe that would be enough to send it away.

Reaching for his light, he pointed it toward the wolf's face and turned it on and off rapidly. The wolf backed away, giving a little yelp. Jake continued, advancing as he went, his arm wrapped behind him to keep Beth close. Moments later, the wolf's tail turned down, its ears flattened and it gave a reproachful yip before trotting away down the path and into the undergrowth. Jake relaxed, thankful the animal hadn't taken too much convincing.

Beth let out a whoosh of breath. Must have been holding it. "I'm glad that's over! When the match didn't light, I was sure you'd have to shoot it."

Jake turned and pulled her into him with his free hand. "I don't think he'll be back. You did great." And she had. No screaming or panicking. Not even a squeak. "Let's keep moving."

Beth's shoulders drooped. She must be exhausted.

"Just a little while longer, we can have a rest soon."

Five minutes later, much to his relief, the track widened ahead. Jake held out his hand and she caught hold of it, walking beside him as they continued. Her steady pace suggested she'd make it, even if blistered feet were the result. They walked on silently, occasionally seeing the headlights of truckers coming from Anchorage.

As time wore on, Jake's thoughts returned to the revelation about Beth. With what he'd learned about her hero worship of Villani, things made sense. If she only trusted Villani, and she hadn't disclosed her status as a protected witness, she probably hadn't made close friends. Without a strong relationship with God—which he had yet to see evidenced—she'd attempt to exercise control over the only matter she could. Protecting her new identity. No wonder she'd taken such care of her appearance. His mind quickly reassessed everything he knew about her. Daughter of poor Baltic immigrants. Teacher and protector of small children. Fearless witness of horrific crime. Even with the seasickness and claustrophobia, the woman was as tough as anything. He'd been dead wrong about her.

Fatigue tore at him, gently eroding the professional barrier he'd created between them. He couldn't stand these thoughts because they only lead one way. Pain. His hand found its way to the gold cross around his neck, and he said the first thing he thought.

"I didn't ask if you were a Christian."

Beth's eyes flicked to meet his for a moment, then returned to the path. "I go to church every Sunday."

He'd been even more wrong about her than he'd thought. "I didn't know that."

"Oh, well, I teach the junior Sunday school group with the help of one of my student's moms. You met her husband, Officer Miller, in Cordova."

"Yeah, I remember." The officer seemed like someone he'd have a lot of time for. "Sunday school, I guess that makes sense with your profession."

"You'd think they'd be sick of me after six days a week." A smile entered her voice. "But I don't get sick of them. I love kids, and I never get sick of that age group—the kindergarten through third grade." She stumbled and he caught her before she could fall. "Thanks."

Jake's stomach knotted. He should keep her talking. "You were saying, about Sunday school?"

"We have a good kids' program at Cordova Community Church, enough for three different age groups on Sunday, as well as the youth group and playgroups during the week." She paused. "What about you? I guess you go to church in Chicago?"

"Yeah. When I'm not on duty." He tried to keep Sundays free, but it didn't always work out. Like this Sunday past.

"You should come along if you're ever in Cordova again." She said it in a matter-of-fact way, but the invitation surprised him.

He hesitated. "Could we pray together? As we walk?"

"Um, sure. You go ahead." The uncertainty in her voice surprised him.

He sent up a silent prayer for clarity, and the parable of the son asking for a fish came to him. Back to the basics of prayer. He spoke aloud. "Lord, thank You for protecting us. Thank You for giving us what we need, even if it is not what we might ask for. Please help me to keep Beth safe. Amen."

If he'd been relying on Beth's answering prayer, he'd have been disappointed. But in his heart, he knew she wasn't going to say anything. They continued for a while longer, the river ebbing and flowing alongside, the Milky Way revealing itself in all its splendor.

Beth's steps began to slow. She must be well past tired. Hard to know how much further they had to go before they reached Palmer, but he guessed they'd been walking for two hours now. The distant lights across the river from what he'd presumed had been the turnoff to the town of Sutton had come and gone an hour ago.

"Do you think God hears us?"

The question surprised him, but he didn't hesitate. "I know He does." Of *that*, Jake was certain.

Beth was convinced her feet were about to fall off. Still slightly soggy, and definitely blistered beyond imagination, she'd never punished them like this before. Not even in the most uncomfortable high heels. How many hours had they been trudging—squelching—along the river? Surely daylight would be upon them soon. That, or at least the town. A hot shower and a warm, soft bed would be nice too. Beth shuddered when she caught a glimpse of a large boulder looming in the middle of the abysslike river. Sore or not, she should focus on being grateful to be alive. Tears pricked her eyes and she blinked them away before they took hold.

Losing consciousness in the water had happened quickly, but she'd still had enough time to watch her life flash before her. Jake's words had rolled around her mind for what seemed like hours. *Lord, thank You for protecting us.* If almost drowning her in the rapids was God's way of protecting them, she had grave concerns for their future. Even so, she envied Jake's faith. He appeared to put everything in God's hands in a way she could not. Between Jake and Pamela, the doubts that came between her and the saving faith her pastor talked about were worth reconsidering. She was still alive, despite the best efforts of the assassins and the river. Was it only down to Jake's skill, or something more?

Up ahead, the path forked, and Jake placed his hand on her shoulder. She stopped and turned to look at him, hoping she'd silently communicated her preference that they stop and rest for a while. Dark rings shadowed Jake's eyes. He must be as tired as she was—and she wasn't even the one carrying the remaining backpack. How she wished she'd thought to grab hers from the car too. At least then she'd have fresh socks. Oh well.

"Go left. I'm sure there'll be a road around here as we get closer to Palmer." He gestured ahead.

So much for a rest. She sighed and trudged on. The animal path widened, like it might be used by hikers. Or moose.

She couldn't stand much more time with her own thoughts, so talking might make things easier. "Are you married?"

Jake grunted.

"I'll take that as a no."

"No. I was supposed to be, but no." The slight catch in his voice suggested she'd hit a nerve. Interesting. Unless his fiancée had died... Beth's stomach dropped. Well, either way, she wanted to talk about it.

"What happened?"

Jake helped her over a fallen log, and the warmth of his rough hand highlighted just how cold hers remained. The silence between them stretched and she thought about asking the question again when he spoke.

"I wasn't good enough."

"What?" Beth leaned forward, her mouth falling open. "I need a bit more than that. Were you actually engaged, or did you just ask and she said no?"

Letting out a long breath, Jake seemed to be considering his words. He'd be within his rights to tell her to mind her own business.

"She said yes. Now she's married to my best—former best—friend." He gave her a look that seemed to say, *Now you know, are you happy?*

"Sounds like you dodged a bullet."

Jake harrumphed.

"What? Who wants to marry someone who doesn't think they're the best person in the world? Imagine being married to someone who thought you weren't good enough. Nothing like a daily dose of stinging criticism to push you into a state of permanent misery."

He sobered a little, raising his eyebrows. "Never thought of it that way."

"*I* think you're good enough." The words left her lips before she'd given them a thought. Heat rose in her cheeks.

Jake gave her an appraising look. "Let's revisit that when you're safe in Anchorage."

Beth's thoughts froze. What did he mean by *that*? Before she could ask any more questions, the bark of a dog sounded in the distance. At least she hoped it was a dog. Her heart skipped a beat. Did wolves bark?

"Come on, let's go." Jake had stepped ahead of her, and

he held out his hand, pulling her along quicker. Her feet protested, but she kept pace.

The dense trees thinned a little and the intermittent barks drew closer. Definitely a dog. Surely, no wolf could sound as happy as that.

They hadn't gone a hundred yards before an Australian shepherd bounded up to greet them, its tail wagging like a feather duster. Jake let go of Beth's hand and crouched to give the dog a scratch behind its ears. "Hey, boy, am I pleased to see you. Is your mom or dad around?" His tone sounded so friendly, Beth's mouth gaped. Could he be the same man?

The dog bounded away, giving excited yaps, and Beth took the opportunity to lean heavily against the trunk of a nearby birch tree.

"Guess he wants us to follow him." The barely concealed relief on his face disappeared when he looked her up and down. "You need me to carry you?"

He must be joking, but Beth wished he wasn't. Her legs were almost as sore as her feet. The only reason the rest of her didn't ache was probably that it competed with worse pain. She limped after him, no longer able to walk normally. His face clouded with concern. "You really could do with a carry, couldn't you? Can you manage a little further? I hope the dog's owner will give us a lift into town."

Beth nodded and didn't protest when he wrapped his arm around her, supporting her as she continued down the path.

The barest shafts of light dawned behind them. Must be the early morning already. Had they really been walking all night? It seemed like way longer than twenty-four hours since they'd boarded the ferry. At least she'd had a little sleep beforehand. But what about Jake? When was the last time he'd closed his eyes. Must be at least thirty-six hours, probably more.

They came to a copse, and the dog bounded back, followed by a sprightly woman Beth guessed must be at least in her sixties.

She raised her eyebrows. "Who've you found, Toby? Lost hikers?" She scratched the dog between the ears and walked briskly toward Beth and Jake. "You two been out all night? You must be freezin'."

Jake held out his hand. "Deputy US Marshal Jake Cruz. Do you live nearby?"

Fortunately, Toby's owner—Maggie Pike—lived less than half a mile away, along with her husband Jim, who gave them something to eat and drink, and let Jake use their phone to call his boss.

"You folks need a ride into town?" Maggie asked.

Jake glanced at Beth. "We'd appreciate that."

A half hour later, Beth sat in the front of the Pikes' faithful banger of a truck, sandwiched between Jim and Jake. The heater blasted in the cab, thawing her feet. They made it to the Palmer PD as the sun rose.

Set on a simple grid, with low-rise buildings mostly one or two floors apiece, the town of Palmer seemed more utilitarian than picturesque at first glance. But the spectacular and seemingly boundless range of mountains, where it sat nestled next to the Matanuska River, offset its simplicity. Beth recognized the towering Talkeetna Mountains to the north, though fog covered their peaks. The Chugach Mountains to the south and east remained covered in snow at this time of year, but the summits of Lazy Mountain and Matanuska Peak peeped through the low-hanging gray clouds where the sunrise reflected.

Jake helped her out of the cab, as her legs had stiffened during the twenty-minute drive. Jim came in with them and introduced them to the desk sergeant before saying his goodbyes.

"You're the folks who've been causing all the trouble, huh?" The desk sergeant raised his eyebrows. "We've had units dispatched to Lion's Head yesterday, with a tour guide caught up in a shoot-out."

"Is he okay?" Beth blurted the question automatically. Poor Ethan.

"He's fine. The assailants took off when the state troopers arrived, but it was too dangerous to pursue them." He turned back to Jake. "We've stepped up the patrols, so if they come back this way, we'll catch them. There aren't too many dark silver Toyota Tacomas riddled with bullet holes on the road."

"Attempted assault on a US marshal is a violation of federal law, so you can expect a visit from some FBI agents too."

"Thanks for the heads-up. The state troopers may want to talk to you as well. I'll notify them that you're here."

Jake gave a halfhearted shrug and touched Beth's arm, gesturing toward some chairs. "Rest your feet, I'll start writing up a report." He barely hid the defeat in his voice.

Beth started for the uncomfortable-looking plastic bucket seats, her muscles protesting each step.

The desk sergeant blew out a breath. "I apologize. You folks must be exhausted. You want to go to a hotel to freshen up? Maybe have a rest while you wait for your ride?"

"You know what, that'd be great." Jake cracked a slight smile and turned to Beth. "Sound good to you?"

The tension fell away from Beth's shoulders. "Sounds wonderful."

An officer dropped them at what looked to be a historic building that had been refurbished as a hotel. Exactly the kind of place Beth Ryder preferred—wood-paneled walls, wingback chairs in burgundies and teals, dark hardwood furniture and lace tablecloths.

Jake got their room keys, then used the hotel's phone to

update his boss. He handed Beth her room key. "Our escort will be here by the end of the day. They've been tied up." His tone revealed he wasn't pleased about it. "May as well get some sleep while we can. Are you hungry?"

Beth's stomach growled in response, and he raised his eyebrows. "How about you freshen up, then we can go get some food."

"Okay."

"A patrol vehicle is posted out front, just in case. We should be safe for now." He escorted Beth to her room, adjacent to his, and cleared it before leaving her in peace.

Beth immediately peeled off her socks to check the damage. Sure enough, her poor feet were red-raw and blistered. Unable to stop the sobs, she let out all the tension of the past couple of days, crying until she had nothing left.

Once she'd cleaned up and changed into the fresh clothes that the woman at reception had kindly provided—including blessedly fresh socks—she rinsed her dirty clothes and hung them up to dry. A knock on the door pulled her away from the fantasy of resting her aching bones on that temptingly plush double bed. The man hadn't even had given her enough time to hide her puffy eyes. Oh well, women cried. He'd just have to deal with it.

"Beth? It's Jake. Are you ready?"

She opened the door, pleased to see Jake had also had a chance to freshen up. "Looking forward to whatever they put in front of me."

Jake smiled, which surprised her. No more grunts? Maybe the sleep deprivation mellowed him. Hopefully not; she'd come to appreciate his abrasive nature had kept her alive. But some small part of her liked his smile.

He'd obtained a phone charger from the reception desk and now plugged it into the power socket next to their table,

placing the phone facedown near the wall. How Beth longed
to call someone—Pamela, anyone—to talk about what had
just happened to her. The enormity of her experience made
her want to simultaneously sob, scream and jump for joy
that she was still alive. A debrief would have to wait. Jake
wasn't likely to handle those kinds of emotions very well.

The breakfast menu looked promising, and Beth ordered
pancakes with bacon, eggs, extra whipped butter and syrup.
Jake chose bacon, sausages, eggs, French toast and fried po-
tatoes with bottomless coffee.

"Don't you want to sleep?" Beth leaned toward him.

"Not until you're safe in Anchorage." He pressed his lips
together, resting his hands on the table. "You should've been
there twelve hours ago. I'm sorry."

Beth reached over without thinking and squeezed his
hand, catching his eye. "Not your fault."

He held her gaze, and Beth's chest tightened. Why did
he look at her like that? Like Officer Miller had looked at
Rachel before they'd… No, it couldn't be the same. She re-
focused her attention on the wood panels, which needed a
light sanding and a coat of oil. When she snuck a glimpse
in Jake's direction, he seemed preoccupied with the pattern
on the curtains.

The waitress came over to top up Jake's coffee. Her wide
smile cheered Beth's heart. "Not long 'til the summer. You
folks here on your honeymoon?"

Beth's heart slowed when a cynical look crossed Jake's
face. Could be remembering his fiancée. Had the woman
hardened his heart to intimate relationships? *Why am I even
thinking about this?*

"No. Thanks for the coffee." Jake's tone seemed more
than a little dismissive.

The waitress left and Beth frowned. "She was just making conversation."

Jake grunted, and Beth's blood pressure rose. Why did he do this hot-cold thing?

"What is with your grunts anyway?" Her own tone came out grumpier than she'd intended.

He let out a deep sigh, then licked his lips. "I am hungry and tired, and honestly, worried about the tardiness of our backup. I don't like waiting."

Beth sat back in her chair. That had to be the most information on his feelings he'd given her since this had begun. Her heart softened. If only he'd talk a little more, maybe they could understand each other. "I don't like waiting either."

"You've been doing a whole lot of that these past couple of years, haven't you?"

"Yeah, I guess I have."

The waitress returned with two steaming plates of food, and Beth's mouth watered. "There you go." She laid the plates on the table, with her signature cheery smile. "Bon appétit!"

Beth considered each delicious element of her meal, wondering where to start. Her fork hovered over the bacon then the pancakes.

Jake bowed his head. "For what we are about to receive, may the Lord make us truly thankful. Amen."

"Amen." Thankful for her waffling, Beth hid her near-embarrassing mistake by sticking a piece of bacon in her mouth. She savored the first salty bite. "Mmm! This is so good!"

Jake didn't even bother with a grunt, halfway through his first sausage.

They ate in silence until Beth finally pushed her plate aside and wiped her mouth. Half a pancake and a sizable portion of bacon remained. "It's so tasty, but I think I may have overordered. Seems like a waste not to somehow force it in, but I'm not sure I can."

"It won't go to waste. I have plenty of room left."

Beth's eyes widened. His portion had been even bigger than hers. "Where?"

"Hollow legs." The twinkle in his eyes sparked something in Beth's heart. How she hoped they'd make it out of this alive.

Jake's heart thudded so hard he was sure Beth could hear it. He hadn't lied about his concern with the tardy backup. But he hadn't told the whole truth either. That waitress's comment about them being honeymooners had sent him off-kilter. Why did he care about the slight sympathy in Beth's face when the word came up? He half regretted sharing about his fiancée. *Now she pities me.* What did that matter? Must be his fatigue. Maybe he could have a quick power nap while she slept. If he couldn't regain his focus, he'd be worse than useless.

Didn't help that her hair had been washed then dried straight. Auburn layers framed her face, bare of makeup and naturally beautiful. Those kingfisher teal-blue eyes searched his like a beacon. How was he supposed to get through the rest of the day? With no distractions, he'd be compelled to ruminate on the memory of those eyes until he drove himself crazy. He could pretend his problem was just her looks, but he'd be lying to himself. Beth Ryder—Karina Baumane—ranked as the most interesting, disciplined and morally upright woman he'd ever met. Her genuine concern for others above herself was a rarity. The sense of justice underlying her testimony should put many self-interested federal witnesses to shame. She'd already overtaken the thoughts of his ex-fiancée, and that fact alone terrified him. *I think you're good enough.* He clenched his jaw. Saying goodbye to this woman could be more challenging than keeping her alive. He had to keep his guard up.

The waitress returned to top up his coffee, slightly less cheery than before. "You folks enjoyin' your meal?"

Jake swallowed his mouthful. "Yes, thanks."

"It's delicious." Beth smiled warmly, her eyes lighting up. "Though I think I overordered."

"You're telling me you don't have room for pie?" The waitress's eyes twinkled. "It's cherry."

Beth swallowed, her eyes widening. "That does sound tempting. Do you do room service? I might need a piece later."

The waitress smiled. "I'll be sure to save you some." She turned to Jake. "Should I save some for you too?"

Sharing a piece of cherry pie with Beth sounded good to him. *No.* Protecting the witness had to be his sole focus. "No, that's okay." Beth's sharp glance caused him to add, "Thanks, though." Great, he was taking his manners from her now? That had to stop too.

The waitress took their plates.

"You ready to go?" He retrieved his phone, winding up the charging cable.

"Yes, thanks to that meal, I'll be asleep before my head hits the pillow."

"After you." He walked Beth out of the dining room, checking for anything suspicious but finding nothing. The lack of engagement with the assassins worried him. They'd managed to track them everywhere, but they weren't *here*? Why not? Maybe the shootout with Ethan had caused them to rethink their strategy. He was glad for the promised USMS escort—it'd be harder to run two armed vehicles off the road.

He accompanied Beth back to her room, clearing it again. Nothing unusual.

"Get some sleep. I'll be in the room next door, but I'll leave my door open. If you need anything, call out." He was tempted to make her leave her door open, too, but that might create more problems than it solved.

Beth yawned. "Excuse me. Yes, that's fine. Wake me up when the escort arrives." She closed the door, and Jake sighed. The coffee hadn't been particularly strong, and his eyes felt scratchy. He stepped toward his room and cleared it as well. Then he sat in the wingback chair next to the bed and pulled out his phone.

His boss answered on the first ring. "Cruz, how are things there?"

"They'd be a lot better if we had a ride, sir. What's the ETA?"

"Five hours. They're headed back to Anchorage now, and they'll freshen up then come straight over to you. How's Miss Ryder holding up?"

Jake's neck tingled slightly. Five hours left a lot of room for trouble. "She's getting some sleep in the room next door. You sure no one else can help? What about the FBI? They must have agents who can transport us. She's *their* witness."

"No." Forsyth's voice sounded sharp. "Sit tight, Cruz. You're safe where you are. There's a patrol out front, isn't there? Are they out the back too?"

"No, but they have units driving by every so often." Why did his boss always micromanage the situation? If he couldn't send backup immediately, there was nothing else to say.

"I'll let you know when the deputies leave here. Call if you have any updates."

Jake ended the call and leaned back in the comfortable chair. He had a good view of the hallway where he sat. No one would get past him without him noticing. He'd rather be outside Beth's door, or better, in the room with her. He dismissed the idea. That would not be appropriate. But he could move the chair closer to her door. Picking up the wing-back, he positioned it in the doorframe. He wouldn't block the hallway, but he'd hear whatever might be happening in Beth's room. Couldn't do much better than that. He sat back, resting his head on the cushion. His eyes drooped.

Moments later—had it been moments or longer, Jake didn't know—he woke, disoriented. A high-pitched beep-ing came from the smoke alarm in the hallway. *Beth!* He leaped to his feet, his heart pounding. Reaching her door, he smelled smoke. Where did it come from?

He banged on her door. "Beth!"

No answer. Adrenaline surged through him, and he banged on the door again, before using the spare keycard. He threw open the door, expecting to see Beth on the bed, but the sheets were thrown back and she was nowhere to be seen!

Jake raced into the room and opened the door to the bath-room. Empty. He searched the room, each closet, under the bed. Nowhere to be found. His heartbeat slammed in his chest like a dodge ball. How had they gotten past him? Then he saw it. A couple of strands of red hair hanging from the edge of the window frame. They'd taken her out the win-dow. *I should've stayed with her.* If he'd been sitting next to the bed, this wouldn't have happened.

If you hadn't been asleep, you'd have heard them.

His throat closed up as he threw open the window. He poked his head out, searching for any sign of her. Nothing, except a ladder pushed up against the wall. Was he too late?

NINE

Beth woke upside down, disoriented and cold. Pressed against something? *Someone?* Her stomach flipped. Was she being carried? Pain throbbed in the back of her shoulder. Her head was encased in a scratchy material that smelled faintly of manure, cattle-feed pallets and cypress. Maybe a burlap bag? Why was she upside down? Her hands were bound behind her back. Her ankles, too, over her socks. No shoes.

She traced her fingers along the plastic-strip restraints that cut into her wrists. Must be like the zip ties Jake had pulled from his jacket. No way she could pull them apart—she'd watched the shooters he'd bound struggle against them to no avail, and they'd been much stronger than she was. She scrunched her face, attempting to remain calm and gain her bearings, even as bile rose in her throat. What had happened? Last she remembered, she'd been asleep at the hotel. Jake had been outside the door. She didn't remember anyone else entering the room. Maybe she remained in the room? Could it be *Jake* carrying her? What a ridiculous thought. He'd never put her head in a burlap bag.

A chill ran down her spine. She must've been taken by Petrov's gang. Why hadn't they killed her immediately? Were they taking her somewhere to do it quietly? Attempting to orient herself, she realized the lump digging into her solar plexus was a person. She had been flung over someone's shoulder! Kicking and screaming wouldn't do her any good. If she had a bag over her head, they were more concerned about her seeing something—their faces, or perhaps her location—than with anyone seeing her. Was that promising? If they were worried about her seeing their faces, maybe they planned to release her. Or maybe they didn't want her to see when they were about to kill her. Despair threatened, and she swallowed it down. No point alerting her captors to her consciousness. Surprise might help her. Maybe she could escape when they tried to load her into a vehicle.

As if she'd willed it, the person carrying her stopped and dumped her on the ground. She ran her hands on the cold concrete surface that seemed to be covered in grit and dust. Unlike anything she'd expected. Unless she'd been asleep for twelve hours, the darkness from the interior wasn't just from the bag. Must be inside somewhere without windows. A room? A hallway?

Maybe it wasn't used often. She wanted to drop something—a clue for Jake. What could she leave behind? She didn't have any jewelry accessible to her hands. Maybe something in her pocket if she could reach it. *If only I could pull it to me.* The chill from the river hadn't left her, and she'd needed to sleep in her jacket. She tugged at it now, bringing the pocket closer to her. *Yes!* Her fingers reached inside, feeling around. The wrapper from Jake's submarine sandwich. She'd shoved it into the pocket thinking she'd dispose of it when they left the car. It had become sodden in the river, but had dried again in her pocket, a lump of paper. Maybe the distinctive red pattern and logo of Pamela's signature takeout packaging would be visible. *Have to at least try.*

Now wasn't the time to drop her valuable clue, though.

Wherever they were didn't seem like a populated area. Maybe when they transferred her? *If* they did.

Two male voices spoke softly, muffled by the coarse material of the bag. Russian? If only she could hear them better. A few more sentences. Definitely Russian, but she didn't recognize the accent. Must be from a different region to her mother. How she longed for her mother. It had been three years since they'd spoken. Would they ever see each other again? Tom had promised that one day they'd be able to visit. Once the last trial had finished. He'd kept Beth updated with what had been happening in their lives. Passed back tidbits from each other's lives that wouldn't mean anything to the enemy. Beth's parents had been forced to move as a precaution, although the OCG didn't seem to have targeted them. Her throat thickened with guilt, and something niggled at the back of her mind.

One of the men bent down and picked Beth back up. If he wasn't from the OCG, why had he taken her? Who were these people? She remained a deadweight, careful to feign unconsciousness. He didn't sling her over his shoulder this time. Instead, he pushed her upward, handing her to his colleague, who pulled her by the shoulders. His bony hands dug into the sinews of her arms. *Where am I? What are they doing?* Her breath caught and she swallowed, hoping they wouldn't notice that her hands had begun to shake.

Her hip scraped painfully against the side of something and she flinched.

"She's awake," the man below called up to his accomplice. Did they know that Russian had been her first language? If not, maybe they'd reveal something that would help her to escape.

I've been so stupid! Beth's stomach contracted. The Bulgarians would *never* use Russians. These men did not work for the OCG! Who *did* they work for?

The man above jerked her onto what might be grass. Light filtered through the bag. Must be outside. The other man joined them, his feet heavy on the ground next to her head. If she'd been taken out in the open, this was her opportunity. Now or never. She released the wrapper from her hands, hoping they wouldn't notice.

"Should we drug her again? I have one more syringe of midazolam."

Beth stifled a gasp. They'd injected her with a sedative. Had they done the same to Jake? Her stomach dropped. Or worse?

"No, better to keep her awake until we get there."

Get where? The sound of a car door opening caused Beth's heart to accelerate. *Please don't put me in the trunk.*

"Stow her in the back seat. I want to keep an eye on her."

Beth breathed a sigh of relief. The head bag was claustrophobic enough without a coffinlike experience.

One of the men picked her up and shoved her onto the back seat. Not high enough for a truck. Must be a sedan. He spoke in English with a Russian accent. "If you try anything, I shoot you in the head."

That answered her question about whether he knew of her Russian language skills. At least one thing had gone in her favor. Maybe they'd say something that would give her an advantage. Although trussed like a turkey, knowing anything about her future probably wouldn't help her.

The car door slammed and the engine started. The vehicle rolled away at a sedate pace, then the indicator clicked for a few seconds before it turned left. Could she remember where they were taking her? Would that help? She needed to try. The indicator sounded again and the car stopped. Then rolled forward, turning to the right. They must still be in Palmer. But where? And where were they heading? From what Beth knew of Palmer, if they headed south, they'd end up in Anchorage. East, they'd end up back the way she and Jake had come, either turning back to Valdez, or eventually hitting Canada. Or west, they could be going anywhere to the north. *I could be on my way anywhere.*

Would Jake see the wrapper?

Jake's blood pressure skyrocketed and he remained momentarily paralyzed at the window. Had they taken her moments ago, or tens of minutes? Should he rush down the ladder or race out front? Maybe the patrol had seen something innocuous that would become important. No, of course they hadn't, because they'd be focused on the fire emergency.

A man with a safety helmet on his head walked into the room. "Sir, you need to evacuate immediately."

Jake followed him from the room and down to the front of the hotel, pulling out his phone and dialing. "Sir." He swallowed, not sure what to say. *The facts.* "She's gone."

"What? What do you mean *gone*?" He deserved every ounce of the fury in his boss's voice.

Hustling out the front door, Jake scanned the crowd, looking for something. Anything. Scores of locals, a handful of tourists, all with necks craned toward the excitement. No one stood out.

"Someone climbed in through the window and took her. Look, I need to go." He hung up before his boss could say another word. He didn't care to hear about the reputation of the USMS, or the implied stain on Forsyth's career prospects. His only care was Beth.

Officers directed the gathering crowd of guests and staff,

who emerged slack-jawed from the building as flames licked its side.

He jogged toward them and approached the female officer. Hoffman. He'd noticed her in the patrol vehicle earlier, and wondered from her facial features whether she might have some Athabaskan heritage. "I'm Deputy US Marshal Jake Cruz. My witness has been taken. Did you see anything before or after the fire that might indicate who's taken her? Any unknown vehicles?"

Hoffman's eyes bulged. "How did they take her? Are you okay?"

Jake's stomach hardened. Naturally anyone would think an assailant would have to overpower a US marshal before they could snatch a witness.

He swallowed his pride. "I'm fine. She slept in her room and I slept outside the door. They got in and out through the exterior window."

"I'll call it in." A look of sympathy flashed across the officer's face. She reached for her radio and gestured for her colleague to come over.

"Thanks." Jake scanned the area, hoping something would stand out. Nothing did. His jaw tightened. Surely the trail hadn't gone cold.

Hoffman turned back to Jake. "We've issued a BOLO, and the chief is dispatching units here to help search."

"Who are we up against?" A male officer in his thirties, with dark blond hair and brown eyes, whose name badge read O'Doherty, frowned and looked Jake up and down.

"A Bulgarian organized crime gang. You know if any security cameras cover the back of the hotel?"

Two fire engines arrived on the scene and firefighters sprang into action. Some unfurled hoses, others rushed toward the burning building.

Jake's chest tightened. "This is a distraction. The fire department can focus on the fire. We need to focus on Beth."

Hoffman nodded. "Got it. There's CCTV in the bakery near the back of the hotel. I know the owner. He'll be happy for us to check it out."

Jake couldn't wait for backup; he had to do something. "Thanks, I'll come too."

O'Doherty walked with them. "So, you think they set the fire as a distraction?"

"I'm sure of it." Jake's fists clenched.

"Then we need to check the security footage opposite the source of the fire. I'll talk to the fire chief and let you know as soon as I have something."

"Thanks."

Minutes later, Jake and Hoffman raced through the door of the bakery, and the warm air hit them right away, along with the pleasant aroma of yeast, sugar and newly baked bread.

"Hey, Mack, any chance we can take a look at your security footage for the past—" She glanced at Jake.

"Hour."

From the flour covering him, Jake assumed Mack must be a baker as well as the owner. "Sure, come on back." He placed his hand on the shoulder of a younger baker, who stood at a bench, basting scrolls with a sugar syrup. "You're on serving duty."

They walked past large mixers, ovens and benches to the rear of the bakery. Bags of flour were stacked to the ceiling next to sacks of sugar. Cakes of yeast and commercial-sized tubs of lard and butter filled the glass-doored refrigerator. Mack rinsed his floury hands under the tap before opening the door to the office.

"Shouldn't take long to scroll back." He logged into the computer and clicked on a camera icon. The screen filled with four views from security cameras. The top left captured the back of the hotel, although the view wasn't detailed— the hotel stood a hundred yards from the bakery, across a block of vacant land.

Jake pointed to the window. "That's the one."

Mack clicked on the image and it filled the screen. He clicked back the timeline one hour. The ladder wasn't in view.

"We're looking for people placing a ladder under that window." Jake pointed to the first-floor window.

Mack fast-forwarded the footage. Cars zoomed back and forth, people entered and exited the bakery from the road. Then two men in hi-vis vests, carrying a ladder, rushed into the frame. Mack paused it, then slowed the footage. The men placed the ladder under the window. The first thing Jake noticed was the men's appearance—they were definitely not the men who'd been following them in the Tacoma. Too tall, and one had bleached-blond hair. The blond climbed the ladder and opened the window, then scrambled through. The second man waited on the ground, looking around as if checking to see if anyone watched them. Then he opened the window on the ground floor and pulled it wide.

"What's he up to?" Hoffman voiced his thoughts, but Jake didn't reply. They'd find out soon enough.

The man returned to the ladder and climbed to wait near the top. The first man returned moments later, with Beth, who appeared to be unconscious. Jake's adrenaline spiked like someone had pulled a gun on him. She wasn't dead! If they'd killed her, they would've left the body. *Lord, thank You for keeping her alive.* The men glanced to and fro, carefully checking they weren't being watched.

The second man reached to grab Beth, slinging her over his shoulder to make his way down the ladder. But instead of walking away, he shoved her through the open window on the ground floor, then climbed in after her. The other man followed, shutting the window after them.

Jake's mind raced. Why would the men want to take her back into the hotel? "When did the fire start?"

"We got the call ten minutes ago, linked to the fire alarm."

He pointed to the time stamp on the footage. "Fifteen minutes. They started the fire *after* they took her. The alarms went off five minutes after they put her through the window."

"Do you think they're still in the building?"

Jake closed his eyes, trying to think it through. "Mack, we need to keep watching your security footage. Can you speed it up again?"

Mack sped up the footage again and they focused on the ground-floor window. Right up until the present time. No sign of the men or Beth.

"They didn't carry her out through the front door. She must still be inside!"

TEN

Jake's heart raced, and he stopped Hoffman, who was headed for the front of the bakery. "Wait here. They may try and bring her back out the window. I'll go check the front of the hotel."

"Okay." Hoffman gave him a frown of barely disguised skepticism. "Let me radio my partner. He can meet you."

"Thanks."

Racing back to the hotel, Jake avoided the fire crew who continued to hose down the building. Familiar smells of smoke and fire retardant filled the area. People had dissipated—only the guests, hotel staff and a few nearby store owners remained. Seemed like the flames had been mostly extinguished.

Officer O'Doherty flagged him over. "Hoffman said you might have found something."

"We think she's still inside." Jake continued toward the entrance.

O'Doherty's voice followed him. "She's not. The firefighters have cleared the whole building."

Jake's heart grew heavy, and he turned to the officer. "Did *you* find anything?"

"Maybe. The fire chief thinks the fire started in a utility tunnel under the kitchen. It's likely they tried to make it look like an accident—a gas leak—but they made a ham-fisted attempt. We're fortunate the whole kitchen didn't blow up."

Hands on his hips, Jake's eyes flicked at the hotel with impatience. "What about my witness? Security footage showed the men deposit her into the ground floor. She hasn't exited."

"If they used the utility tunnels to light the fire, they may have used them to transport her."

"Where do they come out?" Jake's muscles tensed in readiness.

"All over." O'Doherty frowned, thinking. "If I were them, I'd probably want to come out somewhere secluded, with vehicle access." His face lit up. "I have an idea. Come on."

The officer hustled past the hotel, away from the crowd, and toward a parking lot packed with cars that backed onto older residential houses.

Jake's skin tingled. "How do you know about this?"

"I grew up here. There are maintenance tunnels all over for servicing the underground utilities." He paused near one of the old houses, examining the ground. "I think it's around here somewhere." Walking a little further, he crouched. "Yup, here it is. And it's been used recently—it's normally overgrown with grass."

Jake peered over O'Doherty's shoulder. A rusted metal cover with a handle appeared to be embedded in the ground. Lush spring grass sprouted near the gravel of the parking lot.

"I'll call this in, then we can go down." O'Doherty reached for his radio, and Jake searched the area around the opening.

Tire tracks were visible in the gravel but could be from any vehicle—the parking lot appeared popular. A few yards along, in the grass, a ball of paper caught his eye. The distinctive red seemed familiar. Pamela's café. Couldn't be a coincidence. *Beth, you clever woman.*

"You found something?" O'Doherty walked toward him.

Jake pointed to the wrapper. "Looks like it's just been dropped, doesn't it?

"Sure." O'Doherty waited for him to elaborate.

"The café is in Valdez. We ate there yesterday. I'm certain Beth—the witness—dropped it for me to find."

O'Doherty reached for his radio. "In that case, let's hope we can find a camera that points toward the entrance of this parking lot."

Jake pulled out his phone and dialed his boss, who answered with a stern, "Yes," on the first ring.

"Sir, we need to arrange a roadblock. Are those deputies far away?"

"You've IDed the vehicle already?" Supervisory US Marshal Forsyth sounded impressed.

"I'm working on it, but this is our one chance to find her. There are three roads out. One heads toward Anchorage, so our guys may as well cover that one."

"Leave it with me."

O'Doherty ended his call at the same time. "I've asked the Alaska State Troopers to help. Let's track down that vehicle."

Jake's mind swirled with the possibilities. They'd taken Beth alive, even though they could have executed her quietly in the tunnels. Why not kill her? They could make a clean getaway and eliminate the chance of her testifying. Unless that wasn't the reason they'd taken her. But what other reason could there be? Their boss needed Beth out of the picture to ensure he didn't go back to prison. Didn't make sense. His hand found the cross around his neck. *Thank You, Lord. Whatever You're doing to spare her, I am grateful. Please continue to protect her. Please comfort her.* His heart ached at the thought of the fear she must be experiencing. What if they'd put her in the trunk of the car? She'd be beside herself. *Focus!*

"Hoffman's checked the security footage from the gas station across the street. Two men who match the ones you saw earlier left ten minutes ago in a black BMW 7 Series sedan. I've put out a BOLO and updated the troopers."

"Any idea where they were headed?"

"North, but there's a chance they'll double back. Hoffman's going to pick us up, and we can try and catch them."

Some of the tension left Jake's body. "Thanks, I appreciate that."

Moments later, Hoffman pulled up near the hotel. Jake climbed in the back and O'Doherty rode shotgun. Hoffman sped north, lights flashing.

Jake placed his hand on the back of Hoffman's seat. "Thanks for finding that vehicle."

"You're welcome. The state troopers will set up roadblocks this side of Wasilla and Glennallen. Our local officers are coordinating with the Palmer troopers to cover the area. Just in case they don't take main roads."

"I'll let my boss know." Jake called his boss and updated him, then ended the call. "Okay, US marshals are coming from Anchorage. They're about an hour out, so they'll see the vehicle if it's headed to Anchorage." Something in Jake's gut told him they wouldn't be, though.

They left the town and drove north, then east, headed toward Glennallen. The scenery blurred in a monotonous stream of spruce, birch, hemlock and pine. The Matanuska River that had tried to take Beth from him less than twenty-four hours earlier surged momentarily to the right before he lost sight of it again. Grateful he wasn't at the wheel, Jake tried to focus his thoughts on a plan. Instead, the sight of Beth's red hair draped down the back of an assassin replayed in his mind in a haunting loop. Was she awake yet? Had they…? No, she had to be alive. They must be transporting her somewhere for a purpose, otherwise they'd have killed her in the tunnels. She wouldn't have been able to drop him a clue. For the first time in his career, he'd gotten emotionally involved, and it might get them all killed. *Lord, please help me to focus.* He wiped the sweat from his palms.

The radio crackled. The state troopers had checked in at each roadblock. No sign of the BMW.

Jake glanced at the clock on the dash. "They've had a twenty-minute head start. How long until they hit a roadblock?"

"If they're driving the limit, ten, maybe fifteen, minutes." O'Doherty glanced at Hoffman. "You agree?"

"I'm doing my best to gain on them."

"I appreciate it." Jake didn't know what else to say. They could be hurrying in the wrong direction.

Beth's hands had become numb. She'd been wedged in the back seat, facing the front of the car, so she couldn't relieve the pressure on her wrists. The adrenaline had worn off and lethargy had replaced it. Her shoulders ached, her neck prickled uncomfortably and her nose stung from the chafing of the burlap bag.

Jake must have noticed her absence by now. He may have left her to sleep, but she suspected he'd have checked in on her. That thought kept her going. Help might be on its way. How long would it take him to find her clue? If he found it at all. What a long string of coincidences she relied on for rescue.

Her breath bottled in her chest. No, she didn't have to rely on coincidences. Jake was good at his job. She had faith he'd find her before long. He'd pray about it. Maybe God would help him. That thought brought her even more comfort.

While she couldn't see them, she sensed the men were

alert, and worried. They hadn't spoken since they'd started driving. She and Jake hadn't planned to be in the hotel—that had been a last-minute decision. So how had the men found her? How had they known which room? Who'd known where they were? The concierge, the waitress and the Palmer PD. Only the concierge had known which room she'd been allocated, though. Had *he* told these men about her? How had he even known about her? Jake's standard-issue vest might have given them away.

One of the men—Beth guessed the one driving—cleared his throat and spoke in Russian. "It worries me Serge hasn't heard from Bakalov."

Beth's stomach contracted. Who was Serge? Their boss? Did he work for the US senator she was supposed to testify against? That didn't make any sense. Senator Bakalov seemed as likely to hire Russians as Petrov. Or would he go behind Petrov's back? Like Beth, he was half Russian on his mother's side. He could be playing both sides. She'd given a written and video statement to the FBI. If the senator kept her alive, maybe he planned to bribe her to change her statement. Or threaten her with death if she refused?

The other man spoke. "He'll call soon enough. We have what he wants."

"What if he doesn't come through with the goods?"

The goods? Did this mean they *didn't* work for Bakalov? How she wished her head didn't ache so much. Maybe if she could get some more air, she'd be able to think through what was going on.

"Relax, would you? If he doesn't come through, we'll kill the girl ourselves and make it look like the Bulgarians did it. The police don't know who took her. They'll assume it was Petrov's guys. They've been sniffing around all week."

Beth stifled a gasp.

"Hold up, if we kill her, where's our money?"

"Serge will pay us whatever happens. Bakalov's problem is our problem, and Serge'll be happy we solved it."

Payment? Did these men work for the Russian mafia? Adrenaline coursed through her and tears pricked her eyes when she remembered her mother's cautionary tales of the foolish young women from her village who'd borrowed from the mafia to study in America. She'd die no matter what happened.

"I don't understand Serge. Bakalov has to be forced into loyalty to us. Why is this our problem?"

Frustration oozed from the other man. "That's why you're the driver and the muscle, okay? Serge is the boss for a reason. He knows more than we know. There'll be some deal. I don't want to know."

"Okay." The man sounded a little offended.

The other man continued. "We stick to breaking knee-caps, and nobody gets hurt."

"Unless it's your kneecaps." The men chuckled together and whatever tension had been brewing between them dissipated.

A sick feeling rose within Beth. He'd used the Russian word *avtoritet*—authority. The head man of his division. The Russian mafia had captured her.

Beth startled when one of the Russian's phones rang with a shrill octatonic scale. He spoke in Russian. "Yes?" Beth strained to hear the other end of the conversation, but it was impossible. "Okay." He ended the call. "Change of plans. The police have blocked the roads. We need go another way."

The car slowed, then U-turned so swiftly that Beth's body slid along the back seat and her feet smashed into the door. She yelped with pain, and the men chuckled.

"She hasn't suffocated yet. I was beginning to wonder."

Then the man raised his voice and spoke in English. "Don't worry, honey, we'll let you go soon." His hand connected with Beth's leg, and he patted her, sending a chill down her spine. They had no intention of doing that.

The driver spoke in Russian. "Where do we go? My GPS is out of range. I told you we should get better burner phones—this one doesn't have any functionality."

"Talk to Kvasnikoff, he's the one who bought them." The other man paused. "There's a road that will take us the back way to Talkeetna through the mountains. We can have the jet pick us up at the regional airport there, and take us to Bakalov, or wherever Serge wants us to go."

"I didn't see a road."

"Don't worry about it, I'll point it out when we get there. We passed the turnoff maybe five minutes ago."

The driver grunted, reminding Beth of Jake and his endless grunts. What she'd give to hear that sound now. Her throat thickened with despair at the thought of what her death would mean to him. He'd be the first US marshal in the history of the USMS to have a witness killed on his watch. She couldn't let that happen either. It was unforeseeable that they'd take her like this. These men had slipped completely under the radar of the USMS and the FBI. She could only hope that another government agency had been watching their activities, so at least they might discover who had killed her.

Don't think like that, you're not dead yet.

If Jake had got her sandwich wrapper, maybe he'd be looking for other clues. What else did she have she could drop when the men eventually transported her from the car to the plane at the airport? No way she could reach her pockets in this position. Her hands remained unnervingly numb.

Even if she could find something to leave, it seemed like

a long shot. Leaving trash at an airport wouldn't stand out. That left escape. She wiggled her toes. Plenty of feeling— the men mustn't have bound her ankles as tightly. She tested the zip tie and, to her surprise, it loosened. Had the locking mechanism failed? Or maybe they'd tied it incorrectly in their haste? Her belly fluttered, ever so slightly, with hope. If she could pull her feet apart when they opened the door, she could run.

Only, she couldn't see. Could she take the bag off of her head? She dipped her chin, trying to determine whether the bag had been pulled tight around her neck. If she could slip it off… Then what? She'd make a dash for it and hope they would miss when they shot her? *They're going to kill me anyway.* Making a dash for it gave her a better chance of survival than doing nothing.

"There, turn there."

"You sure this is the one?"

The man cursed under his breath. "Yes, I'm sure. Turn!"

The vehicle swerved off the highway and turned onto another road. Beth's wrists squashed painfully against the back seat and bolts of electricity went through her fingers. She bit her lip to stifle the exclamation that would no doubt bring more taunts from the men. At least she still had feeling in her hands, even if it left her in excruciating pain.

"How far along do we go? This looks like it's heading into the mountains." The driver's voice sounded skeptical.

"I don't know, just keep driving and we'll get there. Everywhere here is mountains. May as well be the Kamchatka Peninsula." The men chuckled again.

The journey certainly seemed mountainous, with no straights, just bends. Beth's stomach roiled and she worried what might happen if she became sick again. *I have to distract myself.* She attempted to snag the burlap bag on the seat, but it slid off. The covers on the seats must be made of something too smooth. Maybe she'd have to wait until the car stopped. If only she could loosen her hands.

The driver spoke again. "How long does Bakalov have before we kill the girl?"

"Twelve hours."

"We'd better get to the airport soon, or Serge will have our hides."

A sudden heaviness overcame her. Twelve hours left to live. *Unless I can escape.* She pressed her temple against the seat, tucked her chin into her neck and gently pushed against the material of the burlap bag. After a few tries, a slightly fresher air wafted over her chin.

They'd been going maybe fifteen more minutes, and Beth had worked the bag into a position where her chin was exposed. The car took a hairpin bend, slowed down and rolled to a stop.

"This isn't the way to the airport. It's a dead end!" The driver let out a string of colorful Russian expletives, many of which Beth had never heard before. Her mind raced, and the chill of unease flooded her senses.

"Keep going. There's a sign up ahead."

The car rolled forward and the driver exclaimed loudly. "It *is* a dead end! What's wrong with you? We're going to be trapped!"

The other man swore. "Stop the car. This is too risky. I say we dump the girl down a mine shaft. They'll never find her. Even if they stop the car, there'll be no evidence we had her. We can worry about Serge later."

Beth's heartbeat thumped so hard she was sure the men could hear her. *I have to escape, or they'll kill me and dump my body where no one will find it.*

ELEVEN

Beth's body surged with adrenaline when the car engine stopped. They wouldn't kill her in the car—too much blood. They'd carry her somewhere. She just had to kick them out of the way and run. *Easy, right?*

The men opened the doors, their words blending into a sea of insults. The moment the car lightened from the men's exit, she tossed the rest of the bag from her head and yanked her feet free. Pulling her knees to her chest, she waited. The back door opened at her feet, and she kicked the door as hard as she could. The impact jarred her ankles, and she drew a sharp breath, using it to propel herself upright. Her head spun and she blinked. The man stumbled back, crying out in pain. Beth didn't wait for their reaction, swinging her feet out of the door opening and forcing her body away from the car. The icy air shocked her like a slap in the face. Fog, gravel, vegetation, empty heritage buildings. After being stuck with her head in a bag for so long, the surrounds came like an unrecognizable barrage of images. *What is this place?*

Running with her hands tied behind her back presented a challenge, but she didn't have much choice. The swearing and shouts of the men from behind her were close by—too close. If she stayed on the road, they'd be upon her in moments. She veered into the scrub. Since the covering of fog obscured the view, she hoped it would shield her as well. She had to go up—away from the road. Low bushes scratched at her, snagging her ankles, but she fought on. Moisture soaked through the thick socks and wet her shoeless feet. Hopefully she wouldn't stand on something sharp. A bullet whizzed past her and she gasped. They'd decided to kill her *now*!

She risked a glance behind her. One of the men stood, maybe thirty feet away, his pistol aimed directly at her. The scrub offered no cover, and before she could move, he fired. Pain shot through her upper arm and she dropped to the ground. She couldn't crawl with her hands behind her, and if she stuck her head up again, he'd shoot her. Remaining in place wasn't an option either. Where was the other man? Had he returned to the car?

More shots fired, only not in her direction. Had someone else arrived? Maybe the men from the OCG? She couldn't wait around to find out. When she peeped toward the man, his back was turned. She ran uphill, finding another track among the vegetation. The track ascended steeply as she ran, and the patchy film of mist enveloped her. The men wouldn't be able to see her. If she continued up this track, maybe she'd find somewhere to hide. Shots fired in her direction, but they missed by a wide margin. The men didn't know where she'd gone. That could change if she didn't hurry.

Stumbling ahead, the howl of wolves sounded in the distance. She'd risk wolves before the barrel of a gun. Her legs cramped, the wound on her arms stung and her shoulders fizzed from the effort of running with them splayed behind her. How much longer could she keep going?

You don't have a choice. It's just you.

How she wished Jake were here with her. His presence had made every struggle so much easier. He must be frantic. A new resolve flowed through her, and she picked up her pace. No way she'd let him down by dying.

Ahead the path forked, and Beth paused. What if one of them looped back to the men? She'd be doing their job for them. Her chest tingled from frustration at her indecision as much as exertion. What would Jake do? He'd already be headed in the right direction without hesitation—he had some kind of internal compass. *Up. Go up.* Yes, looping back wouldn't be in an upward direction. Calves burning, and hands tingling from the cold, Beth hastened to the left, hoping the men would take the other path, if they came this way at all.

The vegetation had thinned out and rocks covered the ground, stinging her blistered feet. She tried to relieve them by leaning against a rocky outcrop, but a shard of rock dug painfully into her thigh. She stumbled away from the rocks before realizing the sharp piece of centuries-old, cooled magma, might help her. She pressed the zip tie holding her wrists against the sharp edge. It caught, and she leaned down, applying as much pressure as she dared—no point stabbing herself in the palm. A few more tries, and the bonds broke. Beth's arms sagged against her sides, then involuntarily lifted forward, kind of like the times she and her sister had used a doorframe to levitate their arms. Blood rushed back into her hands, and they prickled uncomfortably.

Beth rolled her shoulders and massaged her wrists. Her arm still stung where the bullet had pierced it, her feet were beyond description, and the aches and pains of the past couple of days were coming back with a vengeance.

She listened, straining to hear where the men might be now. Water trickled in the distance, and any birds or other wildlife that might be around were quiet in the soupy fog. And the guns were silent. There were no footsteps, no voices.

Had they given up? With her hands free, she had a much greater chance of survival. But where would she go? The air smelled of rain, and if the temperature continued to drop, she might be caught in a torrent of hail or sleet. If she followed the track back, she might bump into the men. She could keep going into the wilderness, but where would she end up? Without supplies or even a box of matches, most likely food for the wolves and coyotes. She waited completely alone. *Not completely.*

Thoughts of Jake's faith returned to her. Even with all his training, all his experience, he continued to pray. To rely on the Lord. Why didn't she? What was she afraid of? Her mind returned to Pamela's words. *The Lord isn't done with you yet.* All the people she trusted and respected most relied on the Lord. What held her back? Being let down?

Fog blocked her vision, like the ghostly smoke of a wildfire, and the quiet space of the Alaskan wilderness filled her with apprehension. Could she seek solace in God?

"Lord, I don't know if You're listening. I don't know if You even know who I am. But I need strength to keep going. Please help me. Amen." As she spoke the words, a sense of calm descended over her. She took a few limping steps further along the path and a small alcove appeared in the rock face. Maybe she could wait there. At least it would shelter her from the wind and the rain. Rest her feet.

Beth leaned against the wall, hunkering down in the hollowed-out space. She closed her eyes and finally dared to comfort herself with Jake's words. *Let's revisit that when you're safe in Anchorage.* She sighed. Did she hope he meant what she thought he meant? No, of course not. He was her protector, just like Tom had been. She was making a feeling of security into something it wasn't. *But maybe I'm not.*

* * *

Twenty minutes in, Jake asked Hoffman to pull over. "We'd have caught them by now, we're halfway back to Palmer." Dread growled like a rabid coyote in the pit of his stomach.

O'Doherty and Hoffman shared a look, and O'Doherty spoke. "There are lots of backroads. Plenty of places to wait us out."

"We can start checking road by road, if you want?" Hoffman's tone sounded dubious.

Jake's mind raced and he took a deep breath. The OCG case was a big deal. The FBI could arrive and start a search any time. Unlikely the kidnappers would hang around and wait for that. "Is there any other way they might go?"

"You know, there's a chance they'll try to go via Hatcher Pass. It's only open a few months of the year, but they're not local. They might've seen it on a map and thought it would take them right through to Talkeetna." Hoffman looked at O'Doherty. "You think it's worth a try?"

"Yeah. Good idea." O'Doherty gave Hoffman another look; this time one that Jake suspected showed a little more than professional admiration. None of his business.

"Okay, let's go." *Lord, is she even alive? Please have mercy on her.* The gold cross dug into his fingertips.

Hoffman swung off to a road that wound through residential housing. The weather had turned, and low clouds hung over the glacial-sculpted mountain crags. The bright green vegetation stood out against the rocky soil, with drifts of snow remaining from the last flurry. The patrol vehicle climbed the winding road, and Jake's scalp prickled with apprehension. Would they find the men in time?

His phone rang—Forsyth again. "Cruz, where are you?"

"Heading up a mountain toward Hatcher Pass."

His boss harrumphed. "The state troopers have offered to maintain the roadblock until we find Beth, so I'll send the marshals back toward Palmer. *When* you find her, I'll send them to you."

Jake appreciated the confidence of a *when* not an *if*. "Thanks, sir."

"Your boss?" O'Doherty turned back to glance at Jake.

"He's sending the marshals our way." Jake hoped they'd be quick.

They lapsed into silence and Hoffman navigated the road in the descending fog that curled around the roadside, obscuring the rocky peaks and alpine tundra. If this continued, they wouldn't see the BMW—or anything else—until they were upon it. And that might be very soon, courtesy of Hoffman's impressive driving skills.

Would Beth be out in this weather? Had they removed her from the car? Or could she be somewhere else entirely? He ran his hands over his face, frustrated at how powerless he'd become once the men had taken her. The recriminations could come later. *Lord, I need You more than ever. Please help Beth. Help me.*

"Have you been to Palmer before today, Cruz?" O'Doherty's attempt at conversation interrupted Jake's thoughts.

"No."

"When you get your witness back, you should visit us. We'll give you a tour, won't we, Naomi?"

Hoffman smiled. "Sure. Sounds fun."

Jake wished they weren't so cheery, but he couldn't complain. They were helping him way outside their job description. He might feel the same if so much wasn't at stake. "Thanks, I'd appreciate that."

Soon, the vehicle slowed to the speed limit and they approached the entrance to Independence Mine State Historical Park. Jake had heard about the area, which had been a gold rush village up until the Second World War, after which it became a ghost town. The buildings were mainly double-story structures clad in silvered wooden boards, with gabled and cross-gabled roofs—some more dilapidated than others. Most had letter-box-red window frames with peeling paint. Others had succumbed to the elements, now crumpled, building-shaped piles of boards.

They looped back around the buildings and Hoffman slowed the vehicle, rolling to a stop. "There's the BMW."

Jake reached for his gun. "Do you see the men?"

O'Doherty craned his neck. "No. We'll find them, though."

Hoffman pulled the vehicle around to block the BMW's exit and called in their position to Dispatch. Jake and O'Doherty climbed out of the patrol vehicle and edged toward the BMW. The crisp, cool air was infused with a slightly mildewy scent. Gravel crunched noisily under their boots, like an early alert system. At least they'd hear anyone walking toward them.

Jake peered through the windows. "No one in the car." He opened the door, reached in to grab the keys from the ignition and pocketed them. He checked the back seat, and his gut dropped when he saw the small burlap bag lying on the floor. *Beth.* No blood, which was something.

Hoffman had followed O'Doherty, and they stood in front of the BMW, weapons drawn. Jake approached them. "Are you familiar with the area?"

O'Doherty nodded toward the buildings. "The town is empty this time of year, so they could be in one of the buildings, but this fog is pretty dense. We can clear each building. It won't take long."

"Are there mine shafts?" A chill crept down Jake's spine. From what he knew of historic mines, while most would have been collapsed for safety, the warrenlike network would still run through the mountains like empty veins. What if the men planned to kill Beth and dump her body?

"Unless these guys know the area, they're unlikely to find one easily. I think we should stick to checking the buildings." Hoffman took the lead and walked toward the first building.

O'Doherty and Jake followed.

Shots fired nearby, and Jake's heart plunged. They raced in the direction of the sound, and Jake decided he wouldn't worry about the element of surprise. O'Doherty and Hoffman could handle themselves, and he wanted to distract the men from whatever they might have planned for Beth.

"US Marshals! You are surrounded! Come out with your hands on your heads!"

A volley of gunfire replied.

Lord, please let us draw the shots away from Beth.

Hoffman and O'Doherty spread out, fading into the fog. Jake took cover behind the side of one of the buildings—not that the thin wood would stop a bullet. The men from the security footage raced toward the BMW.

"US Marshals! Drop your weapons!" Jake trained his gun on the men, who tried to make it to their car. But Hoffman had gotten there first, with O'Doherty on the other side. They were surrounded.

One of the men shot at Jake, but O'Doherty fired back, wounding the man in the hip. The other one dropped his weapon.

O'Doherty slammed the man he'd shot onto the hood of the BMW, and Jake grabbed the other one, letting Hoffman cuff him.

Jake wrenched the man to his feet. "Where's the woman?"

The man spat on the ground, and O'Doherty pulled the other man to his feet. "First one to talk gets to wait for the marshals in the patrol vehicle."

The men shared a look and Hoffman shrugged. "Guess it's the gravel for both of you." She took the man from Jake and pressed him to the ground.

Jake turned away as heat rose within him, trying to collect his thoughts. *She can't be far.* "I need to find my witness." He swallowed. "Backup will be here soon. Are you okay without me?"

O'Doherty frog-marched his prisoner over to Hoffman. "Go ahead. We're fine. I'll patch this one up and call it in."

Jake didn't wait for further confirmation, hustling in the direction from where the men had come. He sent his exact position to his boss. The marshals would be there soon, as well as the state troopers. If Beth lay bleeding out somewhere, she couldn't wait. *Lord, thank You for bringing me this far. Please help me find her.*

Sometime later, noise from the rotors of a helicopter woke Beth, along with a voice calling her name. How long had she been out? Long enough to get a crick in the neck. The helicopter sounded farther away, the voice closer. Jake! He'd come to find her!

Beth struggled to her feet and staggered out of the alcove, toward Jake's voice. Tears welled behind her eyelids and a sudden lightness filled her. "Jake!" Her voice came out in a croak, and she cleared her throat, wishing she had water. "Jake!"

"Beth?" The happiness in his voice mirrored hers. "Call out again!"

"I'm here! Right here!" She half ran toward the sound of his voice, tears streaming down her cheeks.

Out of the fog, he came. Ten feet away, closing the gap in seconds. The unexpected joy on his face filled her heart with warmth. He'd found her. Maybe her prayer had worked. *Thanks, Lord.* He gathered her into his arms and held her tight. "I thought…" He sighed into her hair, not needing to say anything else. Beth breathed him in, so grateful for the sweat, gunpowder and stale coffee wafting from him. Then, before she could think, his lips were on hers. Holding nothing back, he kissed her. She melted into his embrace, savoring the closeness. Just when she wondered whether this was a dream, he pulled away, mesmerizing her with his gaze.

"Beth." He stepped back, his eyes wide. "I'm sorry. I shouldn't've—"

A sudden weakness overcame her and a hand went out to steady her, finding the rock behind her. *I'm sorry?* She swallowed, feeling dizzy.

Jake's eyes swept over her to her arm, and his face clouded. "You've been shot." He peeled off her jacket and examined the bullet wound from which blood slowly trickled. Jake pursed his lips and reached into his jacket, pulling out a slim first-aid kit. He quickly secured gauze to the wound with an elasticized bandage. "That should hold it until we get you to the ER."

The faint sound of gunfire drew his attention. "We need to get back. You okay to walk?" He glanced at the blood-soaked socks on her feet. "Oh, wow. Lean on me."

Beth nodded, unable to speak. *He kissed me. And he's sorry?* Her thoughts scrambled. It had been a nice kiss. But it was obviously a mistake in the heat of the moment. Why did he do it? Surely, he didn't kiss every witness he'd mislaid. No use thinking about it now. *Let's revisit that when you're safe back in Anchorage.* Why would he apologize? A mild panic gripped her, and tears threatened. This was too much to take in.

Jake wrapped his arm under her shoulders and gripped her hand, taking much of the weight from her feet. They retraced their steps toward the ghost town. As they reached the fork in the track, the sound of a helicopter's rotors accelerating filled the air. "Can you go faster?" His words held concern rather than frustration.

"I can try."

They sped up their pace, and Beth did her best to ignore the pain shooting through her feet and body. It had become difficult to isolate where the pain came from—everything just hurt. She swallowed, and let Jake guide her. His body pressed against hers reignited her confusion. She couldn't fall for her protector. Questions remained. *Why did he kiss me?* He wasn't an impulsive man. Maybe she'd been wrong about him.

It seemed like much less time elapsed returning to the ghost town than it had taken to flee. Jake's pace had picked up when they'd reached the flatter path, and he'd practically carried her along. While the view was veiled by the misty rain and fog, Beth could still make out two cars parked in the road—a black BMW and a Palmer PD vehicle.

Jake stopped, his arm holding her back. He lowered his voice to a whisper. "This is not how I left them." He licked his lips and edged toward the police vehicle.

A low groan came from behind it. Jake pulled Beth after him, shielding her body with his. They rounded the vehicle and Beth gasped.

Two police officers lay on the ground. The man wasn't moving. The woman had a head laceration and blood poured from a gaping wound in her thigh.

"Oh no, please no." Beth's face drained of color. *If I'd been faster, we could've saved them.*

TWELVE

Jake raced toward Hoffman, pulling Beth after him. "Where are the prisoners?" He grabbed the last bandage from the first-aid kit. The patrol vehicle would have a full kit, but there wasn't time to get it. Hoffman had already lost a lot of blood. She could easily bleed out.

"Took them by helicopter… Professionals… Foreigners." Her words came out in gasps, and she winced when Jake pulled the bandage around her thigh in a tourniquet.

Beth had already taken off her coat and rolled it into a makeshift pillow, easing it under Hoffman's head. Jake handed her gauze and she pressed it against the wound on the officer's temple.

"Where did they land?" From what Jake could see, it would be impossible to bring a chopper down safely in the fog.

"Didn't land." Hoffman's breathing slowed. Her face had paled, and now it turned gray. She'd pass out soon. Where was that backup? "Is Seamus…is he okay?"

Jake glanced over. O'Doherty must be dead. No way he'd survived whatever had pierced his vest—a high-velocity round from an assault rifle, if Jake had to guess. But he wasn't going to tell Hoffman that. Sirens sounded in the distance. "Help's almost here. Hold on, okay?" If the helicopter hadn't landed, how had they retrieved the prisoners? "I need more information, Hoffman. Did they take the prisoners?"

Hoffman blinked slowly. "Shot us…from the chopper." That explained the rifle rounds. O'Doherty hadn't stood a chance. "Two men rappelled down…took prisoners…back up." Only trained professionals could perform an operation like that. If they were foreigners, could this be a foreign military operation? Or were they mercenaries? Didn't make sense if the men were from the OCG. Maybe Beth knew more.

Beth gave Jake a sharp look, then leaned down to Hoffman. "Do you know your blood type?"

The sirens were close by now. That was probably all the information he'd get. Beth was right to prioritize Hoffman's wellbeing. The details would have to come later.

"O positive." Hoffman murmured. "Seamus… AB negative." She closed her eyes.

"Stay with me, Hoffman." Jake shook her. "Hoffman? Naomi?"

Alaska State Troopers, US Marshals Service and Palmer PD vehicles screamed onto the scene with a kaleidoscope of lights. An ambulance brought up the rear. Before they could draw breath, Jake and Beth were surrounded with help.

Jake's admiration for Beth had only grown in the last half hour. Shrugging off her own need to be treated by the paramedics, she'd given Hoffman's stats and blood type like a professional, offered her own compatible blood and comforted her when the officer learned her partner had died.

She didn't complain when the second ambulance had arrived to treat her, even though the treatment of her feet must have been especially painful. The paramedics stitched her bullet wound, unable to convince her to take pain relief. Only now that they'd been stowed in the back seat of the USMS's sports utility vehicle, waiting for the marshals to return to escort them to Anchorage, did she give him a weak smile and ask for some water. What kind of childhood had she had to make her so resilient?

Jake retrieved two bottles from the console, along with some ibuprofen tablets. He opened a bottle for her, noticing her hands were shaking, and held it steady for her to take a sip.

"Thanks." She waved away the pills, wiped her lips and sighed, then relaxed into the seat, looking out the window. "I hope she'll be okay."

"Me too." He reached over and took her hand, giving it a squeeze. "How are you doing?"

Beth gave him a sad smile and pulled her hand away. "Officer Seamus O'Doherty is dead because of me." She crossed her arms and returned to gaze out the window. How wrong she was.

"No, he's dead because of *me*. If I—"

"*You?* How?" Her eyes flashed like he'd offended her.

"I never should've fallen asleep on the job." The crushing sense of failure made his shoulders sag.

Beth frowned, her lips pressed into a straight line. "You hadn't slept for…what, fifty, sixty hours?"

Jake did the calculation in his head. He had closed his eyes for fifteen minutes at Beth's house, but that was the last time. So, yes, around sixty hours since he'd had a decent sleep. Didn't matter. It was negligent to fall asleep. He'd have to deal with the reprimand or suspension—whatever his boss decided to dole out—when he returned to Anchorage.

Her voice softened. "Besides, it's silly to second-guess that. If you hadn't fallen asleep, you'd be so impaired, I doubt much would've changed." She swallowed. "Maybe you'd be dead too."

She might be right about that. He'd be asking his boss why

backup had been delayed for such a long time—he should never have been put in that position.

He touched her on the shoulder. "I accept that, but you need to accept the man who shot O'Doherty is the one responsible for his death. Okay?"

Beth sighed. "Okay."

He couldn't help his gaze lingering on her lips, and he remembered the feeling of holding her in his arms. The relief that she'd survived. But it'd been more than relief. Giving her a hug would be appropriate for the sense of relief. So, what had possessed him to continue on and kiss her? And then to apologize? That apology had been a lie. He wasn't one bit sorry, even though there was no way around his actions being misconduct. He'd be astonished if Forsyth didn't remove him from duty. Even so, he wouldn't go back and change it if he could. This wasn't like the handful of the other times he'd feared a reprimand for misconduct. Rather than fear or regret, he felt lightness. Beth wasn't just a witness to him anymore. Kissing her was worth whatever penalty came his way. *Why did you apologize?* The poor woman must be confused. But it was for the best. The penalty wasn't a problem, but Beth's safety remained critical. It couldn't happen again, or *he'd* be the one who put her life in danger.

He wrenched his gaze from her, focusing on the congregated law enforcement who'd cordoned off the area, negotiating jurisdiction. Shouldn't take too long—the federal crime would take precedence, so the FBI had control of the scene.

The marshals returned to the vehicle, and the driver turned to Jake, who was positioned diagonally behind him. "Why didn't you tell us there was an active shooter? We would've come straight here."

Jake's lip curled and he glared at the deputy. "I briefed

Forsyth every step of the way. Why did it take you more than twenty-four hours to arrive?"

The driver held up his hands. "We're five hours into our shift. You'll need to take that up with Forsyth." He turned back and started the engine. "Let's get you folks back to Anchorage."

Jake's body tensed, and heat flushed through his body. Someone was lying. And if they'd lied about backup, was someone also feeding information to the OCG, or whomever those professionals had been? Who could he trust?

Beth's hands shook and she tucked them under her thighs, feeling a little lightheaded. Must be the adrenaline crash. The pain on Hoffman's face when she'd realized her partner lay dead on the ground came back to her, and her belly knotted. That would haunt Beth forever. She needed to distract herself.

Only, her thoughts couldn't shift from the present. Anchorage wasn't a long way away, probably an hour. But a lot could happen in an hour. Were they safe on the road? The Russians—or whoever had picked up her captors—certainly weren't afraid to kill law enforcement officers. Her heart rate picked up again as she imagined Jake in harm's way. Surely the USMS would give them more backup after what had happened.

As if reading her mind, Jake glanced behind them at the Alaska State Trooper vehicle following and spoke to the driver. "Will the troopers follow us to Anchorage?"

"Yes, a unit from Palmer is following us halfway and an Anchorage unit will meet us and return to Anchorage."

"Good." Jake sighed and settled into the seat, and his eyes lingered on her.

His gaze became a little unsettling. She didn't want to engage with him until she could collect her thoughts. Again, her mind returned to that kiss. *Why* had he kissed her if he hadn't meant to? It complicated everything. Jake's kiss had been better than anything her imagination could conjure. He'd gone back to his professional self now, hadn't he? *That's* why he'd apologized. She tried to imagine any other law enforcement officer she knew kissing her but drew a blank. Maybe his kiss had meant something? Did he like her in *that* way? No, if he did, he wouldn't have said sorry. Besides, hadn't Beth rationalized her feelings just hours ago? He was her protector, nothing more. She sighed. *This sure feels like more.* Sometimes these things were beyond her control. But his finding her had also been out of her control, and he'd done it anyway. She bit her lip. No, it was way too much to ask God for help with her disastrous love life. He had much more important things to do.

Jake gazed out the window at the sun dipping over the pastoral countryside beneath the Chugach Mountains and Pioneer Peak. Was he thinking about their kiss? No, he'd be thinking about his next move. Or maybe that horrible ex-fiancée. Well, to be fair, Beth had no idea whether the woman was horrible—but anyone who'd promise their hand in marriage then revoke it because their chosen man wasn't good enough? At best, questionable. No, that wasn't fair at all. *Think about your own flaws before judging others.* Didn't matter whether that judgment remained in her head. Her jaw tightened as irritation stormed through her. This had to stop. Especially now there were Bulgarians and Russians after her. *Just buck up and get on with it.*

Jake's voice broke into her thoughts. "Beth?" Had he been speaking?

She turned to him. "Sorry?"

"I asked if you knew who took you."

Thankful for the distraction, Beth turned to him. "I think they were Russian mafia."

Jake's body stilled. "What makes you think that?"

"Stuff I heard in childhood." No need to get into the details.

"They didn't know you're a native Russian speaker, I take it?"

Beth shook her head. While she'd desperately like to fall into Jake's arms and sob a little about the fact the men had discussed how they'd kill her, she couldn't. That was the kind of information the FBI might get if it would help the case. No one else. But she could give him something. "I think they have some association with Senator Bakalov. I'll brief the FBI when we get to Anchorage."

Jake's jaw clenched. Was he annoyed she didn't reveal more? Seemed unlikely. He was professional enough to know his place. Retrieving his cell phone, he dialed. "We have a complication. There are two distinct groups trying to take our witness." He listened, and his faced darkened. "No. I'm not letting her out of my sight." He listened again. "I don't care. The danger is worse now. We're in charge of security, *you* meet us at *our* HQ." He ended the call and let out a long, slow breath. "Can you drive a little faster, please? We need to get to Anchorage before dark."

Thankfully, a little under an hour later, Beth and Jake arrived safely at the USMS office in Anchorage.

Two female FBI agents from her case, Special Agent Gregson and Special Agent Chang, greeted them as they alighted from the elevator. Gregson stood a few inches taller than Chang, probably five foot nine, with a strong jawline, dark blond hair clipped short, and a smear of neutral lipstick. Chang had the physique of a body builder, and her long black hair was twisted into a low bun. Unlike Gregson, she paid more attention to her appearance with impeccable makeup and a dark red manicure so perfect Beth involuntarily curled her own ragged nails out of sight.

Beth's shoulders slumped. She had no desire to be interviewed until she'd had a good night's sleep.

"Can we please do this in the morning?" Her voice came out with slightly more despair than she'd intended.

Gregson frowned. "Beth, we need to debrief now. You told Deputy Cruz that men from a Russian crime syndicate are involved now. Is that correct?"

"Yes." Beth sighed.

"We must investigate that as soon as possible. I can see how tired you are. But could you give us maybe ten minutes, please? Then you can go rest and we can follow up in the morning."

Jake stepped forward. "Miss Ryder needs eyes on her at all times."

Gregson looked Jake up and down. "Thanks, I'm aware of the situation. How about you go debrief with your boss?"

He opened his mouth as if he planned to say something, then shut it again and swallowed. "See you in the morning, Miss Ryder."

The FBI's ten minutes turned into an hour, and by the time they'd debriefed her—a debrief that felt more like an interrogation—Beth could barely keep her eyes open. Jake had been pulled off duty to rest, and the deputies who'd traveled with them from Palmer were to protect her overnight.

When Beth awoke the next morning, she could barely move. A coppery taste coated her mouth, and her body ached all over. She rolled out of bed and hobbled toward the bathroom, wincing when her feet hit the cold tiles. She'd been too tired to do anything but fall into bed the night before, thankful the window of her hotel room looked onto a busy street across from the government building where the USMS was headquartered. The deputies who'd seen her to her room had assured her she'd be completely safe. She'd latched the door anyway, had positioned a couple of booby traps under the window, and wedged a chair against the door. Thankfully, none of her precautions appeared to have been necessary.

Once she'd freshened up, she realized her stomach was completely empty. Hunger had deserted her last night, but now it became worse than the fatigue and the pain. The expected zero eight hundred knock on the door startled her, and to her surprise, when she checked the peephole, Jake stood waiting. Her heart leaped, and she instinctively checked her hair in the mirror. *What am I doing?* She couldn't indulge this fantasy any longer. Jake was assigned to her. She was his package. That was all.

She opened the door, and he smiled. "Good morning, Beth. Did you sleep okay?" Not the formal *Miss Ryder.* Maybe because they were alone. He'd recently shaved and smelled of hotel soap and peppermint. Must've been staying in this hotel too.

"Yes." Then she yawned, and laughed, thankful the humor shook out some of her nervousness. Jake didn't seem nervous. Maybe he'd put the kiss out of his mind. He seemed less of a ruminator than her. "Yes, despite the yawn. Is there any chance of breakfast? I'm starving." Least she could do was act normal too.

"We'll go back across the road and have food delivered." He reached for his radio. "The package is on its way."

Beth's heart sank. *Package.* Yup, that about summed her up, didn't it? She plastered a neutral smile on her face and allowed Jake and two other marshals to escort her to the lobby.

They stepped out onto the street, and a black sedan pulled

up. The window opened and the muzzle of a submachine gun emerged.

Jake shoved Beth behind him. "Gun! Get down!"

THIRTEEN

A flurry of bullets spewed in their direction, and Jake clasped Beth to him, throwing them both to the ground.

Beth let out a loud *oof* as she hit the sidewalk.

The other US marshals crouched and returned fire. An Anchorage PD patrol vehicle rounded the corner, flipped on the lights and sirens, and accelerated toward the car, which peeled away.

Thank You, Lord, for Your perfect timing. Jake dragged Beth to her feet and carried her across the street and into the USMS building. A team of marshals raced past them toward the street.

He checked her for injuries, his heart racing. "Are you hurt?"

"I'm fine. Are you okay?" Her breath came out in gasps. "The other marshals?"

Jake glanced toward the scene, catching sight of the deputies who'd accompanied him. They'd backed onto the sidewalk, guns drawn, and at first glance seemed to have gotten away unscathed. "They seem fine."

Beth let out a breath. "Who found me?"

Hopefully, the Anchorage PD would pick up whoever had opened fire, and they could answer that question for sure. But Jake already had his suspicions. The firearm looked and sounded like a Shipka—a standard-issue, 9-millimeter Bulgarian submachine gun. "We'll find out. Don't worry, you're safe here. They won't let anyone into the building." He gave her arm a squeeze. "Let's get you something to eat."

Twenty minutes later, Jake pulled out a chair in the empty break room for Beth. The interior of the room could have been any USMS break room throughout the country, except for the sad-looking prints of Alaskan scenery. The same drab, neutral colors of linoleum, laminate and wall paint. Same brand of coffee machine and coffee. Same acoustic tile ceiling and eye-straining fluorescent lighting. Even the same stale smells of coffee grounds and allegedly "lemon scented" bleach. Jake could do with some fresh air, but that'd have to wait.

Once Beth had settled herself in an uncomfortable molded-plastic chair, he passed her a cup of Earl Grey tea and a breakfast burrito—the food delivery driver deserved a large tip for the hoops he'd had to jump through to deliver it.

She let out a huge breath. "Thanks, I really need this." Pulling the wrapper off the burrito, she took a decent bite and closed her eyes. "Mmm."

Warmth radiated through Jake's chest. How could he explain his feelings for this woman? Wasn't possible. If only he hadn't made such a hash of things. He placed his own burrito on the table opposite her before walking to the coffee station. Hopefully the distance would help him to focus on the job at hand. What would Forsyth's next move be? To keep Beth at a safe house here in Anchorage? Or to move her to Chicago? If it were his choice, it'd be here. While he knew the streets of Chicago best, he suspected Beth would find it harder to be cooped up in the city. But the problem remained that Beth's location kept being leaked. Maybe she'd be safer in Chicago.

He poured a cup of coffee, took it back to the table. Beth's eyes didn't move from her food when he sat, and he gave thanks for that. Only so many times he could avoid being drawn in by those aurora-like pools.

Unwrapping his burrito, he opened his mouth to take a bite. But Supervisory US Marshal Forsyth powered into the room. At six feet and three inches, and around two hundred and fifty pounds, with the countenance of a pro wrestler, the man dominated whatever space he entered. Jake rewrapped his burrito. Hopefully it'd stay warm a while.

"Cruz, let's find an office." Jake had missed the debrief last night. Forsyth had been on an extended private call, and Jake had taken the opportunity to clock off and get some food and a good night's sleep. Jake had updated him over the phone once backup had arrived at the mines, so his boss knew the facts of what had happened. But he hadn't had a chance to yell at him yet.

Jake stifled a sigh. "I'll be back soon. Don't go any-where—or let anyone eat my breakfast." He winked at Beth, hoping it would indicate she didn't need to worry. She'd be safe in the break room. No one would get past USMS security—especially after what had just happened—and Beth wouldn't let anyone move her without some difficult questions.

She gave him a tight smile. "Sure thing."

Something had changed between them. The easy compan-ionship had evaporated, replaced with a stiff professional-ism. Entirely his fault. Upon reflection, kissing Beth while on duty must be the worst decision he'd ever made, profes-sionally. The rules were in place for good reasons. Apologiz-ing was just the icing on the cake. But how could he bring it up with her? *Sorry, it was unprofessional of me to kiss you.* Way worse than an apology. *I should've waited until I was*

off duty to kiss you, then I wouldn't have had to apologize.
A real charm offensive.

He followed his boss down the hall into a meeting room
and closed the door behind him. Forsyth had flown in from
Chicago shortly after Jake had departed Cordova, basing
himself out of the Anchorage office, no doubt hot-desking.

"Take a seat."

Jake slid into one of the meeting chairs, and Forsyth
leaned back in his, a grim twist to his mouth.

"Are you okay?"

He swallowed. "Yes, sir. Miss Ryder's okay, too, aside
from her injuries."

"Good. So. How did you lose her?" His tone sounded
heavy, not angry. Maybe he was building up to it.

"I don't know for sure, sir. Like I told you over the phone,
Miss Ryder slept in a room adjacent to mine. I left my door
open. I told no one outside this office where she was located.
I fell asleep, which I shouldn't have done. The men took her
while I slept."

"You followed procedure. I don't think anyone else would
have had a different outcome."

Jake rubbed his chin, not sure whether to be reassured
or concerned that his boss was so understanding. "Maybe."
Should he share his concerns with him? "Sir, I'm concerned
how unexpected this was. We were on the second floor. I
don't know how they found her room so easily."

Forsyth frowned. "Did Miss Ryder make phone calls from
her room?"

"Not that I'm aware." It hadn't occurred to Jake she might
have given her location away; she'd been so careful about
her identity.

"What do you think happened?"

Jake licked his lips. Did he risk sharing his suspicions

with Forsyth? He'd worked with the man for close to a decade, as a colleague from their junior years and then under him when he'd been promoted to supervisor. Jake trusted him completely. But would he think Jake clutched at excuses for his failure? His ego shouldn't come into it. Beth's safety was paramount.

"I'm concerned someone—a US marshal—may be leaking information."

Forsyth's eyes widened and he leaned forward. "What information?"

"Our location, for starters. Every step of the way, the OCG has found us. Then the Russians. Only the USMS knew our location. Unless you passed it on to another agency?"

Forsyth frowned. "Only when you needed backup. But that was managed out of *this* office. They have the relationship with the local state troopers and PDs."

Then there were the lies. "Well, this office might have a problem. They told you there were no available units, but the deputies who picked us up at Hatcher Pass said they'd only been on duty for five hours. Something doesn't add up."

"You're right." Forsyth's frown deepened.

"How well do you know the team here in Anchorage?"

"Well enough. I'll follow up with the deputies and their supervisor. But I think we need to start keeping things between ourselves until we know where the leak is. I'll accompany you and the witness back to Chicago myself. Is there anything else you need?" Forsyth pushed his chair back.

"The estimated time of departure."

Forsyth stood. "That'll depend on what I hear from the FBI. Stay here for now, and in the next few hours, we'll either book a plane or you can transfer Miss Ryder to a safe house." He held his hand to the door, indicating the meeting was over. Without any yelling.

The relief that Jake had expected didn't come. Instead, a slight unease quivered in the pit of his stomach. He'd expected consequences—at the very least, a stern rebuke. How had he read that wrong? Was he losing his touch? Or was his boss working against him? Jake shook his head. No way. Forsyth had been a committed US marshal longer than he had been, and he cared about his career more than anything else. Always had. No way he'd jeopardize it with subterfuge.

He paused at the threshold. "Is there somewhere comfortable for Miss Ryder to wait? Her injuries yesterday were extensive, and she needs to rest. Especially if she's going to be flying soon."

Forsyth's eyes were back on this phone. "There's a sofa in one of the meeting rooms. Down the end of the hall. I don't think anyone's using it."

Jake returned to the break room. Beth appeared absorbed by her cup of tea, her hands wrapped around the mug, her eyes fixed on its contents. Next to her lay a gun magazine, open at a review of the new Smith & Wesson 10-millimeter M&P. Intriguing. She was either very bored or had an interest in military- and police-issue guns he didn't know about. He watched her for a few moments, considering how he should proceed. Should he talk about their kiss? Probably not until he'd worked out something coherent to say. Or maybe he didn't have to say anything. Could they pretend it didn't happen? No, he didn't want that. Whether or not his actions were unprofessional didn't change his feelings for her. Maybe he'd have to play it by ear. Aside from the fact she hadn't pulled away and slapped him, her feelings for him were clear as fog. Better to stick to work. He cleared his throat, and she startled.

"Sorry, I didn't mean to make you jump."

She smiled, although it seemed forced, and she picked up

the magazine. "No problem. What did your boss say? Am I being moved?"

"Not yet."

Her shoulders slumped a little. "So, we just stay here?"

"Yeah." Jake's stomach growled.

Beth's next smile appeared genuine. "You'll feel better after a burrito. Trust me." She focused on her magazine, flipping the pages. Maybe she wasn't reading it after all.

Once Jake had finished his burrito and his second cup of coffee, he sat back and stretched. How had the Russians known Beth's room number? The question had rolled around his mind since he'd spoken it to Forsyth. Should he ask her Forsyth's question about whether she'd make a phone call? No, it wasn't his place. If the question was worth asking, the FBI would have already done so. But if he were to try to work out where any leak came from, having the bigger picture would help. Should he tell Beth his suspicions? He dismissed the idea. Worrying her more would be the only result of that. No, he had to learn more first.

"How did it go with the FBI last night?"

Beth grimaced. "Fine. They're very interested in the re-lationship between the Russian mafia and Senator Bakalov."

"Understandable. Did you have much to tell them?"

She gave a half shrug.

Jake's throat constricted. Whatever intimacy and trust they'd shared on the journey to Anchorage had dissipated. Beth had locked her armor back in place, and probably her heart with it. Maybe he should've asked an open-ended ques-tion. Normally it wouldn't be necessary with Beth. She was good at sharing. How could he get her to open up to him again?

Maybe he had to pray about it.

* * *

Beth's gut swirled like a whirlpool. Why was Jake being so nice to her? This wasn't like the man she'd met in Cordova. The mixed signals were doing a real number on her emotions. Best to stay neutral. Only, how could she when their kiss played like a loop in her mind? She forced her eyes to return to the unoriginally named *Gun Magazine* she'd found in the break room. Not that she'd absorbed one word of it.

Jake had been quiet for a while now. He seemed deep in thought, his head bowed. Should she have told him what she'd told the FBI? Hardly seemed worth the effort. At the end of the interview, she'd heard Gregson say something about a red-eye back to Chicago, so she assumed whatever information she'd provided was enough.

Would Jake be taking her to Chicago? Probably, since he hadn't been relieved of his post yet. Sitting next to him on a plane for six hours would be torturous. Her thoughts returned to Tom. Things had been much simpler with him. Tom didn't do things to her heart like Jake did.

The temptation to ask God for help rippled through her, but she squashed it down. God was for emergencies only. Yesterday, He had served her well, and she was thankful for that. No way would she push the friendship.

Jake stood. "I'm guessing you'd like to put your feet up for a bit."

Beth's eyes widened involuntarily. The pain in her feet remained, even when she'd relented and popped the ibuprofen. "Good guess."

They walked down a hallway and into a large meeting room decorated with the same drab neutrals as the rest of the building. At one end, an informal area had been designated, with a beige pleather sofa, two matching armchairs and a coffee table. Jake arranged some cushions against the arm of the sofa so that Beth could sit comfortably with her feet up. He sat in one of the armchairs closest to her feet.

"How's that?"

"Great, thanks. Sure beats the kayak."

Jake smiled, and Beth's heart did a little flip. Maybe it *would* be safer to talk to Jake about the case.

He didn't give her the chance. "I shouldn't have kissed you. It was very unprofessional."

Heat rose in her cheeks, and she imagined the embarrassingly bright beet-red that must be gathering momentum to shine like a beacon of shame. "I—"

Jake held up his hand. "But it wasn't a mistake. I…" He drew a deep breath and looked down, kneading his hands. "I shouldn't have apologized like that. I wanted to kiss you." His eyes met hers with a gaze so intense she had to look away.

A flutter of hope filled Beth's belly. Did he really mean it? Could his feelings be real? No, his wanting to kiss her was not the same as wanting a relationship with her. *Listen to his words for once, not your feelings.* The first thing Jake said just now? He shouldn't have kissed her. This sounded a lot like another apology. A sudden heaviness descended and she swallowed, risking a glance in his direction. "Then, why did you apologize?"

He leaned forward, his forearms resting on his knees. "I don't know. I guess an instinctive professional reaction. But—"

"I understand." Beth didn't need to hear any more. She needed him to be professional. To focus on protection, not a complicated personal relationship. "We should focus on the case. How about I tell you what I told the FBI?"

Jake frowned and opened his mouth to speak, but Beth stopped him.

"Senator Bakalov and I have one thing in common. We

each have a Russian mother. The FBI became very interested when I told them I suspected my captors were Russian mafia. They would've explored the Russian connection already, but maybe his mother hid the details well. I'm sure she had plenty of practice at subterfuge during the Cold War—my parents certainly did." Her mind returned to her parents, and her jaw tensed. *Don't get sidetracked with emotion.*

"It's hard for the FBI to get family information from Russia. I'm sure they think that his mother's connected to the Russian mafia, and he's on their payroll. They're probably right. It always struck me as suspicious that his family could afford to educate him at an elite American boarding school when he'd campaigned on being from a working-class immigrant family. His website is vague about a scholarship, but at best, they'd have to pay half. Now I wonder if his mom has a cousin, or a brother, in Russia and they've been bankrolling him. What do you think?" She caught her breath.

Jake's face had sobered, and he pressed his hands to his temples. "You could be right." His voice remained quiet. "How do you know about his school?"

Beth's insides quivered. Thankfully, he'd stopped talking about their kiss. "I looked up everyone I would testify against. It's right on his website. Then I checked the school website. Tuition is currently sixty thousand dollars per annum. Even with a half scholarship, it's not exactly pocket change." She swallowed. Had to keep talking. "I mean, with Petrov and the Russians throwing bribes around like candy, of course the FBI are going to be suspicious about a senator. It's not unheard of for politicians to take bribes, is it? Why would Senator Bakalov be any different? He's a first-term politician. If his family took Russian mafia money, or he's taken money for his campaign, they own him."

"But he works for the Bulgarians—Petrov. How can he work for both?"

The same question had been swirling around Beth's mind since the Russians had kidnapped her. "I don't know for sure. But the men who took me said that whatever was good for Bakalov was good for their boss. My guess is that Bakalov is working for the Russian mafia against the US government *and* the Bulgarian mob."

Jake frowned. "So, Bakalov is the key."

"I think so, yes. I do wonder if Petrov knows that the senator he thinks is in his pocket is working against him. That'd be pretty dangerous for Senator Bakalov."

"You told the FBI all this?"

"Of course. I'm sure they've probably worked it out themselves a while back, but they didn't have enough evidence." She sighed. "That's where I come in. Now I can testify to the Russians' conversation, it's even more incriminating for Bakalov." *And dangerous for me.*

Concern clouded Jake's face. "Beth—" His words were interrupted by the door to the meeting room opening.

Jake's boss entered the room. "Senator Bakalov is about to be arrested by the FBI. They want you to take Beth to Chicago immediately. Once he's arrested…" He gave Jake a meaningful look. As if she couldn't read between the lines too. Once the FBI arrested Bakalov, the clock would start ticking. The Russians and the OCG would be after her with relentless fervor until she was dead.

Will I even make it to Chicago?

FOURTEEN

Six hours on a plane with Jake. Beth's stomach flip-flopped like halibut on the deck of a fishing trawler. She gripped the edge of the sofa. Any benefit she'd gained from resting her feet was canceled out by the tension that bunched her shoulders. They'd be served an on-flight meal, but other than that, there'd be no distraction from the conversation Jake obviously wanted to finish. Wasn't even plausible for her to close her eyes and sleep—it was midday. If only she'd held on to *Gun Magazine*.

Maybe he'd let her grab something once they'd cleared security. Anything to prevent him picking up the conversation. She'd seen that look in his eye when she'd changed the subject. *Let's revisit that when you're safe.* He wouldn't let it go.

A tiny part of her didn't want to let it go either. But hearing that Jake's instinctive reaction to kissing her had been to apologize was such a stab in the heart she didn't want to expose herself to more.

Jake's boss continued. "I loaded your bag into the car with mine, Cruz. We're ready to go. Do you need anything, Miss Ryder?"

Beth shook her head, but inside she rejoiced. Jake's boss would come too? What a relief! Maybe he could sit between them.

She followed Jake to the elevator, her feet burning with each step. He placed his hand on her arm and followed Forsyth, who stepped into the basement parking lot. Two government vehicles stood ready for departure. Jake helped her into the back seat of the second vehicle and slid in beside her. Forsyth rode shotgun.

Outside, the sky remained gray, with high clouds and a slight dampness to the air. Traffic had picked up, and cars parted to let them through—the patrol vehicle that had been waiting at the entrance of the parking lot cleared the way. In total, three USMS vehicles chaperoned them—one with Forsyth, Jake and Beth, the other two serving as escorts. They reached the airport in ten minutes, and the US marshals walked them through the terminal to security. A voice over the loudspeaker announced the gate numbers for each flight, and a line of passengers waited at check-in. Some hurried toward security, where the line grew.

Jake's hand never left Beth's arm, and he kept her between him and the other marshals, glancing every which way. They didn't check in, instead heading directly to security. Although this was a procedure Beth had become used to, the slight clench in her gut recalled the anxiety of that first time—when Petrov had put out a hit on her. As expected, the TSA guards knew they were coming, and once the marshals showed their badges, a TSA guard showed them through a side door that bypassed the security checkpoint.

The extra USMS deputies left Beth, Forsyth and Jake to walk to the gate alone. Jake bent low to Beth's ear. "No one can bring a weapon past this point except us. The danger isn't gone, but we won't get shot at."

At least that was some good news. The stitches in Beth's arm gave a little fizz in remembrance of being shot a day earlier.

Forsyth stopped. "We have a little over an hour before the flight leaves. I need to make some calls. I'll meet you at the gate in twenty minutes."

"Okay." Jake placed his hand on Beth's biceps and walked along the shiny, tiled thoroughfare toward the gate. Announcements continued over the PA system, drowning out the muffled sounds of jet engines departing and landing. The smells of airport coffee and fast food wafted over them, and disembarking passengers streamed past toward baggage claim. Alaskan memorabilia, framed pictures and plaques littered the airport, drawing Beth's attention. But Jake didn't pause for anything, not even the stuffed moose.

Beth's eyes raked the newsstand. "Can I stop and buy a magazine, or a book, please?"

Jake didn't break his pace. "We need to go directly to the gate."

No point arguing when he'd made up his mind. Beth kept walking, her feet becoming more tender with every step. What she'd give for a foot spa right about now.

They reached the gate and Jake directed Beth to a seat closest to the boarding area, slightly isolated from the other passengers. "We wait here for the plane to be ready, then we board before everyone else."

Hopefully she wouldn't need the bathroom—he'd probably tell her to hold it.

He remained on his feet and faced the oncoming passengers, most of whom walked on by to gates farther down the terminal. His face remained neutral but held a hint of a threat for anyone who might try to cross him. That suited Beth just fine. With his attention elsewhere, she could consider how she'd get through the six-hour flight without any reading material. Hopefully, she could request headphones for the on-board entertainment and she could block him out that way.

Stepping toward her, he placed a hand on her shoulder, sending a tingling sensation through her chest. "You doing okay?"

"Yeah." She swallowed. "I just want this to be over with."

He gave her a sympathetic look that dissolved when a middle-aged man, carry-on bag in one hand, phone in the other, went to sit within ten feet of them.

Jake gave him a hard stare. "Choose another seat, sir."

The man did as he was told, and obviously Jake's voice had been loud enough that the other passengers sat as far from the boarding area as possible. Not that there were many—with just under an hour until their flight departed, only five passengers had arrived at the gate. A couple of elderly women, probably tourists, and a woman with her baby in a sling. None posed a threat.

"I'll stay with you until you testify." Jake's words cut through her thoughts. "I won't let anything happen to you, and I won't leave you until you're safe. Then we can revisit what we talked about."

Beth's eyes narrowed. There it was. Those words she'd been dreading even as she'd hoped for them. Why did Jake put her in this position? Would this change of heart toward her last? It seemed too good to be true. She turned away, fixing her gaze on the plane taking off. *You sure have gotten yourself in a pickle, haven't you?* What would Pamela say? How Beth longed for her friend. She'd give her a pep talk and a sandwich and send her on her way. Probably wasn't even that mad about her car.

Beth glanced at the screen showing their flight time. Boarding for regular passengers in twenty-five minutes. She guessed *they'd* board in twenty—that seemed to be the procedure. The crew must be cleaning it and replenishing the catering and fuel.

As if reading her mind, Jake spoke. "Won't be long now. The flight crew are due here soon, and we can make introductions."

Something in his voice put Beth on alert. He seemed nervous. Before, when he'd been on the job, he'd barely spoken to her, let alone told her in detail what would happen in advance. Was this to do with the change in their relationship? Or did he have something else on his mind?

His eyes darted around, and he appeared deep in thought. Surely, his boss would be here soon.

She sighed. They'd made it to the airport safely. *Just have to get through the next day or so.* Once on the flight, she'd be safe. Then, back in Chicago, they'd keep her in a safe house. She would be back to what passed as "normal" for a protected witness. Tom would've recovered by then. Would he pick up the job from Jake?

The discomforting ambivalence rumbling in her belly suggested she didn't know whether that would be a welcome scenario or not.

Jake couldn't shake the sense of foreboding that had settled in his gut. Something niggled at him, but he couldn't put his finger on what. Beth's reaction to his ham-fisted attempt to open up about his feelings had stung. But that had been his own fault. Each time he talked about their kiss, he dumped kerosene on the bonfire he was making out of any relationship between them. That wasn't the feeling that bothered his gut, though.

He checked the surrounds. His boss hadn't returned. He'd said twenty minutes, and it had been thirty. What calls couldn't wait until they landed in Chicago? Jake wasn't concerned about protecting Beth on his own. He'd just prefer a second set of eyes right about now. *What's bothering me?*

This level of unease didn't come to him often. The last time had been when he'd found a couple of empty beer bottles in his ex-fiancée's bin when he'd emptied her trash after dinner. His former fiancée didn't drink beer. She'd accused him of interrogating her. He should've listened to his gut then, might've spared him the embarrassment of another month believing they were going to be married.

Another passenger arrived—a businesswoman dressed like she'd just stepped out of a meeting. No threat. She carried a striped bag with a college insignia on it. *That's* what bothered him. That expensive boarding school Bakalov had attended. Beth hadn't said the name of the school, but something about it…

"Do you remember the name of Bakalov's boarding school?"

Beth tore her eyes from the tarmac and raised her eyebrows.

He focused on her lips, willing himself not to get distracted by her eyes.

"St. Luke's. Why?"

Jake's shoulders sank. Surely it was a coincidence. "Do you know what year he graduated?"

"Two thousand nine." She frowned. "What's this about?"

The same year as his boss. Jake's heart raced. Supervisory US Marshal Forsyth and Senator Bakalov had been at school together. Why hadn't his boss mentioned the connection? Had his suspicions been justified? Could Forsyth be working against them?

The man had always come across as a loyal US marshal. They'd worked together for most of their careers. The idea of Forsyth helping someone beholden to the Russian mafia did not compute. The FBI would've done background checks. He must've been vetted. They would've put all this together. All publicly available information. No way they'd put their sole witness for two important trials in the path of a US marshal who could compromise her safety. Perhaps there'd be another explanation. Jake wasn't privy to the higher-level decisions. Could Forsyth be working with the FBI to trap Bakalov?

Still, as coincidences fell into place with alarming clarity, it didn't explain Jake's gut. It didn't explain why the FBI would allow Forsyth to put Beth into such grave danger. Beth could've been killed so many times in the past few days. Didn't seem plausible the FBI would send her and Jake alone to battle it out in the wilderness.

Conversely, if Forsyth *had* been working with Bakalov without FBI involvement, he'd have been able to send all the hostile parties—Bulgarian and Russian—their way. It'd explain how the bad guys kept finding them so easily. Forsyth was the only one who Jake had informed of their every move. The lies could come from Forsyth as easily as from the Anchorage office. It'd explain the confusion of the marshals in Palmer. Forsyth could've deduced which room Beth had stayed in at the hotel in Palmer and informed the Russians. Jake had given the man every last scrap of information available. Could Forsyth have used it against him?

Lord, I need Your discernment. Please help me.

"Is everything okay?" Beth's eyes had fixed on him.

He'd become distracted, his fingers on the gold cross at his neck. He let it go, returning his hand to his holster. Looking around the passenger lounge, he noticed Forsyth heading their way. Could Beth be in danger from his boss?

"Jake?"

Jake pressed his lips together. No time to share his suspicions with Beth or to take her somewhere else. He'd have to get the truth from Forsyth without alerting him.

"You've finished with your calls, sir?"

Forsyth nodded, looking through the window to the tarmac. A plane taxied toward them, and passengers milled
nearby, eyeing the marshals and keeping their distance. Others filled the seats, keeping a wide berth. The ground crew
would arrive soon.

His boss cleared his throat. "Cruz, how about you go get
some refreshments for the journey? I'm sure Miss Ryder
could do with a magazine as well."

Beth's face slackened with relief. "I'd love a magazine."

Jake's gut contracted. If they boarded the plane to Chicago, it'd be difficult for Forsyth to try anything. Was he
attempting to prevent that from happening? Did he plan to
take Beth somewhere else if Jake left? "I don't think this
is the time to separate, sir. They'll be calling us on to the
plane shortly."

His boss pursed his lips. "There's plenty of time. Here—"
He reached into his wallet and pulled out a hundred-dollar
bill. "Go get some sodas and magazines, would you?"

Jake's heart rate quickened. Forsyth had a reputation for
being particularly tight-fisted, yet he was waving around a
Benjamin?

"No, sir. I think I'll stay here." Jake kept his voice even.
No point drawing attention to themselves in public. They
were far enough away from the other passengers that they
couldn't be overheard.

Beth glanced between them. "I… I can go too. I'm sure
they won't leave without us."

Forsyth ignored her. "Cruz, do as I ask. Consider it a direct order."

Jake's chest tightened. He'd never disobeyed a direct order
before. The penalty for a first offense was removal or reprimand. Forsyth could remove him on the spot and replace

him with another US marshal—it might buy his boss enough time to take Beth somewhere else if that was his plan.

Lord, what do I do? His gut told him to stand his ground. Other than the nefarious reason of wanting Jake out of the way, there were no reasons for Forsyth to insist on such a ridiculous order. He had to stay with Beth, just like he'd promised. "I'm staying with the witness."

"You're looking at a removal, Cruz. You want to do that for a can of soda?" Forsyth's tone had softened, like Jake was being unreasonable.

"Yes, sir. There's no reason for that order." He swallowed. "Unless there's something you want to say?"

Forsyth's face clouded. "What are you talking about?"

"Senator Bakalov, sir. Your classmate."

Beth's eyes widened, and she leaned closer to Jake. "Classmate?"

Jake placed his hand on her shoulder, and Forsyth moved his hand to the holster of his gun. Would he really pull his weapon in a public area? Security cameras would pick it up and TSA agents would swarm in an instant. Homeland Security would be close behind.

Just then, the pilot and cabin crew arrived. Forsyth forced a smile, relaxing his hand against his leg.

Jake flashed his badge. "We're transporting a protected witness to Chicago. Ready to board whenever you're ready for us."

The pilot gestured toward the desk where a woman from the airline seemed poised to make an announcement. "Just give us a moment, the ground crew will send you through shortly."

"Sure thing." Jake took the opportunity to pull Beth to her feet and place himself between her and Forsyth. He then moved toward the airline desk. His muscles tensed. Who could help him? If he made a fuss, Forsyth would pull rank and explain Jake was out of line. They wouldn't immediately believe Jake, that was for sure. Had Beth pieced the situation together? She'd balked at the mention of Forsyth being classmates with Bakalov. Must've realized where he was going with the train of thought.

Her face had paled and she'd pressed her arm against Jake, perhaps happy for him to be in between her and his boss.

"They're ready for you, now." The flight desk attendant smiled, interrupting his thoughts. "If you make your way through the doors, there, and down the jet bridge toward the plane, the crew will greet you."

"Thank you." Forsyth stepped forward, gesturing for Jake to go first. In a physical fight, Forsyth would probably win. Jake had to keep Beth away from him.

Jake pressed Beth in front of him, keeping his eyes on Forsyth. The buzzer to open the door sounded and he pushed it open, ushering Beth through. The door swung shut and he reached for his pistol. But before he could pull it, Forsyth had yanked Beth from his grasp and was holding his gun to her temple.

Jake opened his mouth to yell, but Forsyth beat him to it. "Call attention to this, and I'll put a bullet through her head."

Beth's face crumpled, breaking Jake's heart. He had to get her away from Forsyth.

"What are you doing?" Jake kept his voice low and edged toward them.

"Cuff yourself to the handrail." Forsyth held out a set of handcuffs—of course, it would've been too much to hope he'd let Jake use his own, for which he had a key.

Maybe he could delay, keep him talking. The cabin crew would be expecting them. When they didn't arrive, they'd radio back to the desk. Someone would come through that door. "What's your plan?"

Forsyth's jaw clenched and he grabbed Beth by the hair, pulling her head back until she gasped in pain. "Now! Both hands!" He shoved the muzzle of the gun under her chin and backed toward the exit that led down to the tarmac. No way Beth would survive a gunshot, and if Forsyth really was working for Bakalov, Beth's death was inevitable. If he could just keep her alive a little longer, maybe she had a chance.

"Okay, okay." Although every fiber of his being screamed at him to refuse, Jake cuffed one wrist, dropped the other between the rail and the wall and cuffed his other hand. What else could he do with that gun to Beth's head?

"Drop your gun on the floor and kick it to me."

Jake could barely reach his holster, but he maneuvered his hands toward it and complied.

"Now, your radio and phone."

With more jiggling, wrists burning from the contortions, Jake complied. Forsyth stomped on the radio and phone until they were unusable.

Forsyth bent to pick up the gun. "If I hear you call out for help, she's dead. Understand?"

"Yes."

Beth's pleading eyes filled him with helpless fury. *Lord, in my weakness, I need Your help.*

FIFTEEN

Beth's last glimpse of Jake almost undid her. He'd never appeared so helpless. Or betrayed. Her heart had melted when he'd risked his career for her. Disobeying a direct order so he could keep her from a harm she didn't even know existed—that he'd *guessed* existed. If he'd had proof, he'd have immediately called the FBI, wouldn't he? Maybe she wasn't just a package to him. The cold barrel of the gun pressed against her throat. No point speculating. She had to escape.

What did his boss want with her? Jake had mentioned that Forsyth and Senator Bakalov had been classmates. Didn't take much to understand the implication. If Jake's boss was friends with the senator, he must be taking her to Bakalov. Or any one of his allies. A chill ran through her at the thought of the Russians, or Petrov's people, getting their hands on her. They wouldn't just kill her, they'd make her suffer. She swallowed the bile that rose in her throat. *I'm not dead yet.* She'd have to save herself. Again.

Forsyth ushered her down the stairs and onto the tarmac. The cold air chilled her lungs.

"Hustle." Forsyth's pistol dug into her ribs, and his arm gripped her biceps so hard it hurt. He stopped to let a catering van drive past.

Beth opened her mouth to shout out, but Forsyth stabbed the gun into her.

"Don't try anything, Miss Ryder. There are things worse than death."

What did this man have to gain from betraying his country? Petrov, a violent gangster, wouldn't have much to offer a US marshal, and the Russians would demand absolute loyalty—something she doubted would interest Forsyth. Did he want power? Had Senator Bakalov promised him something he couldn't refuse? Or maybe the senator was blackmailing him. If they'd been at boarding school together, perhaps Bakalov had some evidence or knowledge of wrongdoing that would destroy Forsyth's career. The reason probably didn't matter; Beth was in trouble either way.

A vehicle pulled up next to them, and a ground crew worker in a hi-vis jacket climbed out, pulling on work gloves.

Forsyth flashed his badge. "I need to use your vehicle for official business."

The worker seemed unimpressed. "You need training to drive on the tarmac. Ask for an escort." He adjusted his ear protection and walked away.

"Really." Forsyth's jaw clenched and he propelled Beth into the front seat, climbing in after her. "Dimwit." The worker had left the keys in the ignition. Forsyth backed away, following the yellow lines designated for ground crew vehicles.

Beth willed the worker to notice, but the man had his eyes on his job. She looked around for something she could use. No tools, not even a pen. She surreptitiously reached for the door handle. Maybe she could bail out of the vehicle and run for it?

Forsyth held his gun toward her. "Stop thinking about escape."

She swallowed. Would Jake be coming after them? The vehicle traveled away from the terminals in the direction of the hangars. Did Forsyth plan to take her on a light airplane? Surely, Jake would've alerted the authorities by now.

A private jet taxied toward the hangars. Could she alert the pilot?

Forsyth's phone rang and he answered. "Yes. I'm almost there." He listened, and Beth strained to listen to the other side of the conversation. She couldn't even hear the voice, let alone enough to determine the accent. "Yes. You can take her straight away." He hung up, then dialed.

Beth's stomach turned. Would she end up on a private plane to Russia? If they had a Gulfstream, they could get her to Moscow in nine hours and change. Once she'd left US soil, the FBI would never get her back.

"Serge, I have the package." He listened, then hung up.

A chill ran down Beth's spine. She had no doubt that Serge was the boss—the *avtoritet*—of those two Russian mobsters who'd kidnapped her and tried to dump her body in the mines. If he was talking to Serge now, who had called him earlier? Serge's lieutenants? Would they take her to Serge to finish her off?

The vehicle slowed, and Forsyth turned toward the private jet Beth had her eyes on. Not a Gulfstream, so not Moscow. Tears filled her eyes, but she sniffed them back. *Jake, where are you? Lord, why aren't You stepping in?*

Forsyth turned to her and gave her an appraising look. "You're a very valuable little package, did you know that?"

He'd used that word twice. All fear of Jake believing she was just a package evaporated. Her commodification at the hands of this man was the opposite of her humanity in Jake's. And commodities were to be used then disposed of. She definitely wasn't going to get out of this alive. Not when she could identify him. Nothing left to lose. "Who are you working for?"

A snort came in reply.

"I know I'm not going to live much longer." She swallowed. "At least tell me what's going to happen next."

Forsyth parked the vehicle just inside the hangar and pulled her out. "Walk." He pushed her ahead of him, his gun still pressed against her rib cage, and Beth stumbled along, attempting to take in all the details of her surrounds. Where were all the workers? Surely there'd be engineers or other technicians hard at work? This hangar appeared devoid of human life. Maybe that's why he'd chosen it.

Beth's hands shook, as much from cold as adrenaline. Must be around fifty-five degrees today, before the substantial windchill factor, and Beth didn't have a coat, let alone gloves. At least she hadn't been restrained this time. Was Forsyth confident she wouldn't give him any trouble? Or did he not want to draw attention to them? Who was she kidding? The man was a mountain of muscle. He could do what he liked with her.

He stopped in front of a large tool cabinet that hung open, most of its shelves taken out. The gun pressed to her back as he pushed her forward. "Get in."

Beth's gut churned. "What?"

Without another word, he shoved her into the cabinet and slammed the door behind her. A lock clicked.

Fear tore through her as the tiny space appeared to close in around her. "Let me out!" She banged on the door as well as she could, sandwiched between the front and the back of the cabinet.

Liquid sloshed around the base of the cabinet and the smell of kerosene overwhelmed her senses. Was he dousing the area in jet fuel?

"If you don't pipe down, I'll light a match." The menacing tone confirmed her fear.

Beth shut her mouth, pressing her arms against her sides. Would she burn to death? Tears pricked her eyes.

"I'll meet you at the plane."

Forsyth must be on the phone.

The sound of footsteps receded, and Beth's mind raced. There must be a way out.

"Lord, I don't understand. What do you want from me?" Despair coursed through her. "I'm putting my faith in You. Will You help me understand?"

Tears of frustration ran down her cheeks. Why was she waiting for an answer? None was coming.

Would the tool cabinet offer her any protection? Or would it act as an oven and roast her alive? She couldn't just wait and cry, she had to do something. Forsyth had walked away, so she could examine the interior without the fear that any slight noise would incur a consequence. A few shards of light peeked through the ventilation slits, and it wasn't as dark as she'd first thought.

Beth slid her hand across to the lock and jiggled it quietly. No way she'd be able to open it without a tool of some kind. Her maneuverability was restricted to her arms. She couldn't even crouch down. Running her hands along the wall, she found a loose piece of metal. Could that act as a shim to jimmy the lock? Easing it into her hand with the utmost care, she pulled her hand back toward her. Yes, that might just do it. She pressed the shim into the lock, attempting to lever the latch toward her. Only, it wouldn't budge.

She repositioned the shim and gave it a jerk, but it dropped to the ground with a clang. Her heart sank. Would she be able to retrieve it? Bending her knees as much as possible, she attempted to lower herself, but her hips became wedged. She was stuck! Nowhere near close enough to reach the shim.

More footsteps, and Forsyth's voice echoed toward her, countered by an unfamiliar voice—another American. Could it be Bakalov?

Jake watched helplessly as the door swung shut behind them. How long had Forsyth been working against the USMS? The man he thought he knew had seemed a loyal US marshal. He might be more ambitious than Jake believed was healthy, but Jake had always figured that kind of ambition was for the good of the country. How two high-ranking public servants—a supervisory US marshal and a senator—could betray their country filled him with a mixture of disbelief and vertigo.

Worse, they'd involved an innocent witness who had more bravery in her left hand than the two of them put together. What did Forsyth have planned for Beth? Would he palm her off to Bakalov, or did he plan to use her as a bargaining chip? Both options would end badly for Beth unless he could intervene.

Lord, please keep Beth safe until I can get there to help her.

Jake slid the handcuffs along to the first handrail fastening. The screws should come loose if he applied enough force, but how could be break the rail free when it was fastened in several places? He could worry about that once he'd loosened the screws. Yanking and jiggling the rail, the screws loosened ever so slightly. He gave another yank, but before he could make more progress, a flight attendant power-walked toward him, confusion marking her face.

"Deputy... Cruz?" Her eyes caught the handcuffs, and her

mouth gaped. The woman could go either way—calling the TSA on him or for him. Had to tip her his way first.

"Would you mind radioing for help, please? My witness has been taken by force."

The flight attendant composed herself and reached for her radio. "Of course."

"Do you have a phone I can use?"

The flight attendant pulled out a cell phone, unlocked it and handed it to Jake, even as she spoke into her radio. "We have a Code Bravo, Gate C4. I repeat, Code Bravo, Gate C4." Bravo meant a general security alert.

Unable to lift the phone to his mouth, Jake dialed the FBI main line using the speakerphone and asked for Special Agent Gregson.

Doors opened, and the ground crew Jake had observed at the gate rushed toward him. The flight attendant called out to them. "Do you have bolt cutters?"

One of the ground staff nodded. "I'll be right back."

Special Agent Gregson finally answered and Jake explained the situation, while the airline staff listened in with an unprofessional level of eagerness.

"How long have they been gone?" Gregson's voice hardened.

"Five minutes. I'm going after them. Can you send in a team quietly? Last thing we need is two dozen TSA and Homeland Security agents storming the scene. If we spook him, he'll kill the witness."

Gregson remained silent for a moment, then cleared her throat. "Cruz, whatever you do, do *not* kill Bakalov. I need him alive, even if that costs us Beth Ryder. Got it?"

The flight attendant gasped, sharing a scandalized look with the remaining ground crew member. So much for confidentiality.

Jake's chest tingled. "Got it." Even as he said the words, he knew in his heart if he had to choose between them, Beth would come out of this alive. *Lord, please don't make me choose.*

A man in a hi-vis vest rushed back with bolt cutters, followed by the ground crew member, two TSA officers and an Anchorage PD officer.

Jake held the handcuffs while the bolt cutters did their work. He directed his words to the TSA officers. "I need you to secure the area until the FBI arrive. They have primary investigative authority, so follow their directions. *Do not* use your initiative on this, wait for their instructions." He pulled his hands free. "I'm going to retrieve my witness." He pulled his emergency gun from the ankle holster and transferred it to his hip. His boss had slipped up, not thinking to check if he'd retained his backup weapon. *Thank You, Lord.*

"I should come with you." The police officer stepped forward. "I'm Officer Murphy. Anchorage PD."

Jake pursed his lips. He wanted to slip undetected into whatever situation Beth was in. The more people involved, the more difficult that would become. Still, if he had an officer with him, he could report back the location. Maybe even watch his back. "You willing to follow my lead?"

Murphy inclined his head. "Just here to help."

"Come on, then." Jake rushed for the door, followed by Murphy.

They raced down the steps, and a worker approached them. "Officer, a man made off with my vehicle."

Officer Murphy glanced at Jake, his eyebrows raised meaningfully. "Did he have a woman with him?"

"Yeah, they were headed toward the private hangars. I told the guy he had to have training. At least an FAA authorization, you know." The man shook his head.

Jake stepped closer. "The man is a criminal. We need to catch him. Do you have another vehicle we can use?"

The worker frowned with skepticism. "Who are you?"

"He's a US marshal, this is a federal case. Any chance you can help out?" Murphy's friendly tone had a slight edge that made the man take notice.

"Sure, but you could probably jog faster than I can find you a vehicle. Go around Concourse B, then head east until you see some light aircraft."

Jake didn't wait but raced in the direction the worker had pointed.

"Stick to the yellow lines!" The worker's voice echoed after him, but Jake ignored the instruction, heading around the second concourse. He soon saw the hangars the worker must've been referring to. Past Concourse A, the buildings couldn't be more than half a mile away.

Murphy kept pace with him, his head darting around to check for planes. "Air traffic control is not going to like us out here." His radio crackled.

"Too bad!" Jake increased his pace, running the most direct route across a minor landing strip.

How long until Forsyth handed Beth over? Would he be too late? A jet engine deafened him as it landed then taxied toward the private hangars. Could that be Bakalov? The FBI should be arriving at the airport soon. Then he'd have backup.

Lactic acid fizzled in his legs as his muscles complained from the sprinting. He slowed to a jog, holding up his hand for Murphy to slow down as they neared the first hangar. Jet fuel and engine oil wafted to him, and he pulled his gun.

Keeping his voice low, he leaned toward Murphy. "I need you to hang back and watch. If Forsyth is here, I'll let you know. You then radio back to let the FBI know, okay?"

"You sure you don't want me to come with you?"

Jake frowned. "Forsyth is smart. The chances of me making it past him undetected are near zero. I need to put myself between him and the witness and having you there, too…" Jake didn't want to insult they officer by telling him he'd be in the way.

"Reporting back is the priority, and I can't do that if I have a gun in my face. Got it." Murphy patted Jake on the back and melted into the periphery. What a relief the officer understood without further discussion.

Jake continued, pressed against the wall of the hangar. The smell of jet fuel seemed stronger than he'd expected. Maybe the jet was being refueled. He glanced around the corner of the hangar, which appeared empty. The jet had taxied next to the second hangar, and he crept closer to get a better look.

Jake crouched out of sight when a man in a dark suit and sunglasses, with close-cropped brown hair, hand on the weapon in his jacket, stepped out of the jet, checking for danger. Must be a security detail. No hand or neck tattoos. Didn't look like a Russian or Bulgarian mobster. Could this be Bakalov's bodyguard?

The man stepped out on the steps, followed by Senator Bakalov. Jake recognized him from his file photo. His expensive suit, shiny shoes, carefully coifed brown hair and strong jawline seemed fitting for his position of power. But the man was a traitor to his country, and Jake wasn't about to let him hurt Beth. He shuffled toward the second hangar, remaining in the shadows. A second personal security operative, in an identical suit and sunglasses to the first, followed Bakalov. Forsyth must be there too. Perhaps in the second hangar. But where'd he stashed Beth?

Jake stayed low and peered around the open door into the hangar. Sure enough, Forsyth reached out his hand to

Bakalov, who took it in his. The security detail stood a little way back, checking the area. Jake remained hidden from their gaze.

"Nick, it's great to see you again." Forsyth's face wore the genuine smile Jake rarely saw.

Bakalov nodded; his face grim. "You have the woman?"

"Yes, she's safe. Now, let's talk business."

"I need to see the witness first. Then we talk." Bakalov's voice didn't seem as friendly as Jake would expect if he and Forsyth were old friends. Had he been correct in his guess that someone was being blackmailed? Maybe Bakalov had something to lose, not Forsyth.

"No. I need assurances and then I'll take you to her."

Breath whistled through Bakalov's teeth, and he took a step back. "You said I could take her straightaway. What is this?"

Forsyth glanced behind Bakalov, like he was waiting for someone. The glance lasted a split second, but it was enough for Jake to take notice, and most likely Bakalov too. Had Forsyth involved someone else in this? Was Forsyth actually working undercover for the FBI? Could that explain his actions?

Jake's pulse raced. No, there'd be no reason to keep Jake in the dark at this point. Forsyth knew from Jake's actions that he could be trusted, and he'd had every opportunity to ask for his help. He'd done the opposite. Forsyth had something else up his sleeve.

By the time Jake had processed this, Bakalov's security guys had already placed their hands on their weapons and taken a couple of steps toward their charge.

"What have you done?" Bakalov's voice came across more irritated than concerned.

Forsyth's chin raised just slightly. "You're not the only one interested in the witness. She's a valuable commodity."

A chill ran down Jake's spine. If he didn't find Beth soon, she'd be in bigger trouble than he'd imagined.

SIXTEEN

The powerlessness of not knowing where Forsyth had stashed Beth niggled at him like the whine of the idling jet engine. He knew for sure she wasn't on the plane the senator had just disembarked, but that was about all. Had Forsyth left her in the vehicle he'd taken? Jake glanced at it, then dismissed the idea. Beth wasn't a petite woman, and any cavity would be too small for her to hide. He couldn't inspect the offices at the back of the hangar without revealing his location, but that didn't matter. His boss would be too smart to stash her there. Bakalov could've simply disarmed him and grabbed Beth without a problem, if that were the case.

Nothing else stood out. The ceilings were open and high. The ground was made of concrete. The storage cabinets in the hangar that hung open were chock-full of tools and shelves. Nothing indicated the cabinets that appeared locked would be any different. Couldn't stash anyone bigger than a toddler. Maybe Forsyth had dumped her somewhere on the way to the hangar. He'd certainly had the time.

Jake wracked his brain, trying to recall what he'd seen on his run over that might feasibly hide her. Though he hadn't paid a lot of attention, vague snatches came back to him. Concourse A—no, that wouldn't work, someone would've discovered her by now, each concourse was a hive of activity. In one of the trucks parked near the hangars? Unlikely. Those could be moved without warning. Maybe one of the light airplanes? Same problem. Forsyth couldn't possibly risk his leverage being removed without notice. Seemed much more likely Beth remained close by. Somewhere Forsyth could hand her over and leave before the FBI came on the scene. He must know Jake would be discovered quickly, and he'd had little time for anything elaborate.

Forsyth's words continued. "Sure, if I hand over the witness, I get fast-tracked to assistant director. But I've been offered something even better."

"What's that?" Bakalov's voice held thinly veiled skepticism.

A black sports utility vehicle approached from the hangar behind Jake. He wedged himself next to an air compressor and peered out. Not the FBI. He could make out three men in the vehicle—two in front, one in back. It came closer, and Jake's fists clenched involuntarily. The driver was one of the men who'd shot and killed Officer O'Doherty back in Palmer. One of the two who'd escaped in a helicopter. He caught a glimpse of the man in the back—no one he recognized. The Russian who'd been shot must be laid up recovering. This similar-looking man had likely replaced him. Jake guessed the third man who rode shotgun was Serge. He had that look about him—the slicked-back, dark brown hair, overweight, dressed in an open-necked, button-down shirt, with the glowering confidence of someone in charge.

The vehicle stopped a few yards from where Jake hid, and the driver who'd kidnapped Beth stepped out, his gun trained on Forsyth. His colleague came around and opened the door for Serge, who clambered unceremoniously from the front seat and lumbered toward Bakalov. He said something in Russian that Jake didn't understand, and Bakalov raised one eyebrow.

"Serge." Forsyth stepped forward, as if to greet an old friend, but the Russian merely sneered at him, giving an unmistakable one-word direction to his men. Even a non-Russian speaker would understand Forsyth was in deep trouble.

Jake could not stand back and watch his colleague die. Even if Forsyth were a traitor, he was a US marshal first. Innocent until proven guilty.

He stepped out from behind the air compressor. "US Marshals! Get down on the ground! Now!" When they began to turn, he opened fire on the Russians without hesitation, shooting each of the two goons in the center mass before they could fire their weapons. No point shooting Serge—the FBI would want him unharmed. As for Bakalov, he remained a sitting US senator. An unarmed one at that. His men could be Secret Service, for all Jake knew—their guns might be trained on him, but their fingers remained beside the triggers, not on them.

Jake leveled his weapon on Serge. At this point, he prayed Murphy had heard the gunfire and radioed for help. *Lord, even if I die, please save Beth.*

Serge pulled his own weapon, but Bakalov called out. "Stop. I have enough problems without a dead US marshal. He's obviously alone. Forsyth, cuff him for now, and let's get this deal done quickly." He turned to Serge. "What's this about a side deal? You think you can double cross me without any consequences?"

"You work for me." Serge almost spat the words. "I have every right to make my own deals. I want to hear what this FBI witness woman has to say about Petrov. Unlike you, she won't lie to me." He sneered at Forsyth. "Why not kill the rat while you have the chance?"

Bakalov frowned, like Serge was an annoying gnat, nothing more. "Alexei's in charge now, not you."

Serge's face paled slightly, but Jake didn't get a chance to examine it further as Forsyth advanced.

"Put your weapon down, Cruz, or I'll shoot you myself." Forsyth's cold eyes betrayed nothing.

Jake did as he said. What else could he do? He was outgunned. Maybe Forsyth would stash him with Beth. Holding out his hands to Forsyth, he gritted his teeth while his former friend tightened handcuffs around his wrists.

He couldn't stop the words slipping out. "You're a disgrace."

Forsyth ignored him and forced him to his knees. "Don't give me any trouble, Cruz, and maybe you'll walk out of this alive."

What an obvious lie. Unless Forsyth had something else up his sleeve, he must know that Jake would testify against him. That any deal Forsyth had with Bakalov would mean nothing with Jake's and Beth's testimony. What did he intend for Jake? Words came to Jake then, unbidden. *I am with you always, to the very end of the age.* The end of the book of Matthew. Jake felt a wave of calm descend. No matter what Forsyth had planned, his Savior was with him.

Jesus, please be with Beth too. She needs You more than she knows.

Jake's voice and gunshots startled Beth. She stood up sharply, dislodging her hips from where they'd been wedged. Prickles crept unpleasantly down her legs as they woke from their cramped position. Other voices now, not Jake's. American and Russian accents.

Waves of fear ran through her stomach. Why wasn't he talking? Had he been shot? Never in the time she'd been with him had Jake been shot. He'd always been doing the shooting. Surely, this time was no different. The man she'd come to know seemed indestructible. Time and time again he'd evaded those who'd meant her harm. Even when they were outnumbered and underresourced. He wouldn't take an unnecessary risk. Not one that might get him shot. Not when he still had to find her.

Her stomach clenched; the pangs of fear turned to nervousness. What did her fear for Jake mean? For one thing, it forced her to acknowledge she was more afraid for him than she was for herself. Since this ordeal had begun, Beth had never been afraid for her protector. Not Tom, nor any other US marshals or FBI agents. Not even Jake. Sure, she'd *hoped* they'd be safe. But she'd never had this visceral desperation about their wellbeing. Until now. Her fear for Jake's safety had another dimension she didn't want to admit but could no longer deny. If he died, she would never get the opportunity to revisit all the things he'd promised they'd revisit. Her words about him being good enough. The words she'd been avoiding because they'd meant way more than the flippant comment she'd intended. Jake could see through her, even if he couldn't express it eloquently. He understood her feelings, and despite the lies she told herself, it didn't scare him. And in her heart of hearts, she wanted to revisit things too.

Now the situation threatened to deprive her of the opportunity to see things through. More than anything, she wanted to revisit the fact he was well beyond good enough. He'd proven he was more than her protector. His kiss had suggested it. His selfless actions had confirmed it.

Beth couldn't pretend any longer. Her knees weakened at the thought of him. She loved his grunts in place of words. She loved his care for her that went beyond his duty as a US marshal. She even loved the bungled explanation of his kiss that she'd refused to give the benefit of the doubt. She loved him whether or not he could protect her. Even if he failed.

You don't have to rely on him alone. The words hit her in the heart. Jake hadn't said them, but he might as well have. His faith had sown seeds in her that were beginning to sprout. Even after years of church attendance, she'd never truly appreciated that she had a Savior who could offer protection from death. Who could ease her burden and allow her to rest. Whose yoke was easy, and Whose burden was light. Jake had been relying upon that Savior the entire time, and He hadn't steered him wrong once. Perhaps it was time Beth turned to seek rest in this gentle Savior, whose humbleness of heart would help her to find rest for her soul. Jake's Savior. She loved Jake, and she was ready to trust in the One he trusted in.

She closed her eyes and prayed. "Lord, I beg Your forgiveness. I've taken Your love for granted for so long, and I am truly sorry. Please help me to turn away from my past sins and draw me toward You." Tears ran down her cheeks, but a lightness filled her. Her burden had been lifted. "Lord, please protect Jake. Amen."

Blinking back her tears, Beth listened. Still, no sign of Jake. The other voices grew slightly closer. Not Jake's. Were they coming for her? Had Forsyth killed Jake, and would he now kill her? *Lord, I need Your strength more than ever.*

She grasped around for another weapon—anything that might slow him down if he tried to take her from the cabinet. *I've been ready before. I can do it again.* Her Savior would help her through, no matter what the outcome might be. Finally, she was sure of that.

Her fingertips brushed against something. A screwdriver? She strained to reach it but only succeeded in pushing it further away. Frustration threatened to overtake her emotions and she forced it down. *Your Will be done, Lord*. Whatever that might be.

Footsteps accompanied the voices, which she recognized as Forsyth, Bakalov and a Russian. What plan did Forsyth have for her? Would he hand her over to Bakalov? Or was she about to be traded to the Russians for abuse worse than death?

"She's in this cabinet." Forsyth's voice must be twenty yards away.

"Is that jet fuel?" The Russian's voice held confusion.

Forsyth scoffed. "Insurance."

"Crazy American." The Russian muttered in Russian, and only two sets of footsteps proceeded—the Russian mustn't trust Forsyth. Neither did Beth. But that meant she would be handed to Bakalov. Her blood ran cold. Would he kill her on the spot or take her to his Bulgarian associates? Hard to know whether they'd be worse than the Russians—Petrov's treatment of the wife he supposedly loved didn't bode well for the federal witness who'd put him in prison.

A commotion and running feet overwhelmed the next words of the men. "FBI! Hands in the air!"

Forsyth swore under his breath, and the distinctive click of a lighter sent a jolt of dread through Beth's chest. The hiss of flame taking hold preceded the whoosh of the fuel igniting then racing toward her. *Lord, my life is in Your hands*.

The moment Forsyth had led Bakalov and Serge toward the first hangar, Jake had quietly staggered to his feet. Bakalov's men followed at a slight distance, and Jake seemed of no concern to them as he shuffled after them. Serge's men writhed in pain, and to Jake's surprise, no one seemed intent on helping them. Were they so expendable to their boss? Did

Serge plan to drive himself away without them? Or would the helicopter return to rescue them?

Putting that out of his mind, Jake crept after the entourage and into the hangar. No one stopped him, and by the time the FBI special agents announced themselves, he'd come within twenty feet of Forsyth.

But it wasn't until the flame raced toward the metal cabinet that Jake realized Beth was inside! His stomach curdled as he took in the scene. Shelves leaned up against the cabinet, which is how she'd been able to fit inside. Forsyth must've removed them, or maybe the cabinet had been emptied already. How long had she been in there? How was she coping with the claustrophobia? Looked like there were ventilation holes, so hopefully she'd been able to breathe okay. Until now... The fumes from the burning chemicals could easily suffocate her before the heat reached her. Adrenaline coursed through his body. He'd found her, but could he save her in time?

The cacophony surrounding him rose to a crescendo. FBI agents stormed onto the scene. Bakalov's men closed in to protect their charge, hands hovering near their weapons as if waiting for the senator's instructions. Serge rushed past Jake toward his vehicle at an ungainly lumber, and several special agents dashed after him, guns drawn. Burning kerosene and naphtha assaulted Jake's nostrils, and black smoke billowed toward the ceiling of the hangar.

Jake didn't allow himself to become distracted by the mess. His priority was Beth. He sprinted toward the halon fire extinguisher located nearby. Hands cuffed awkwardly together, he had trouble unclipping the extinguisher from the pole to which it had been attached. Why weren't the FBI agents stepping in to help? Didn't they know their only witness was about to be roasted alive?

No time to get their attention. He dragged the extinguisher toward the fire as precious seconds elapsed. The scraping sound of the metal on concrete was barely audible above the noise.

The heat of the fire reached Jake as he grew near, and his gut contracted. Fires fueled by kerosene-based jet fuel could reach temperatures of over eight hundred degrees in moments. Even if Beth could breathe once the toxic combination of carbon monoxide, sulfur dioxide, nitrogen oxides, volatile organic compounds and other chemicals starved her lungs of oxygen, she might not survive the heat. The metal doors would protect her some, but she didn't have long.

Jake aimed the nozzle of the extinguisher at the base of cabinet and squeezed the release. Liquid shot toward the flames, followed by a sharp, acrid odor as the chemicals did their work. The fire was doused in less than a minute. *Thank You, Lord.* Jake swung the fire extinguisher and broke the lock. He grabbed the handle of the smoldering doors, searing his hands in the process, but he ignored the pain and yanked the cabinet open. Beth stumbled from the cabinet, gasping for air. Her arms and legs were free, and her footwear protected her from the still-steaming floor. To Jake's shock, she appeared completely unharmed. Not even a singed hair.

Jake panted from exertion. "You're okay." Didn't even need to be a question. She *was* okay.

A smile broke out on her face, and she leaned against him, her head on his shoulder. "Yes. I'm fine."

Thank You, Lord.

Before he could ask anything more, strong hands clamped down on Jake's shoulders. Forsyth. "I got him. Here he is. Trying to finish her off."

What? Jake swung around. Two senior FBI special agents eyed him, and Forsyth pulled him away from Beth.

"He tried to sell your witness to the Russians. But I caught him in the act."

Jake's mouth gaped at the audacity. "He's lying!"

Beth stepped forward. "Jake's right. His boss is the one who took me. He planned to hand me over to the Russians. Or to the senator. He's a traitor." The last sentence rang out during a lull, and everyone turned to look at them.

The two FBI agents who'd been talking to Bakalov's security detail turned toward Beth, and Jake realized Bakalov had been watching him and Forsyth. His expression remained unreadable.

Forsyth's face turned bright red, and he pointed his gun at Beth, his finger on the trigger.

Jake didn't think twice. With a prayer on his lips, he threw his body between Forsyth's gun and Beth as his boss pulled the trigger.

Pain radiated from the bullet wound in his gut, and he fell against Beth. More shots fired, but Jake's consciousness faded.

Lord, keep her safe.

SEVENTEEN

It took Beth a moment to realize that the warm, viscous liquid soaking her blouse was Jake's blood. Time slowed when Supervisory US Marshal Forsyth turned his gun on her. Jake had leaped into the path of the bullet, and landed heavily on her, knocking the wind from her chest.

He whispered something, but she couldn't hear because by that time the FBI agents had shot Forsyth in the chest and the gunshots had temporarily deafened her. Was Forsyth alive? He'd been wearing a bulletproof vest. But so had Jake. Must've hit him below the vest.

Bakalov and his security detail had already been hustled away by more FBI agents, and sirens wailed in the background. Beth cared for none of that; only Jake. He'd lost too much blood. Her whole body was soaked with it, and a numbness crept through her chest. Had she been shot too? Surely not. She'd be in pain, wouldn't she?

Before she could think further, paramedics arrived. They carefully moved Jake to a gurney, intubated him, hooked him up to an IV bag and wheeled him into the ambulance. A gnawing worry took over and she barely registered a female FBI agent help her to her feet, wrapping a blanket around her.

"I'm Special Agent Dawson. Let's get you to the hospital."

"I'm fine, I don't need medical attention." The words

didn't sound like her voice, even though they came from her mouth.

"You're in shock." Dawson helped her into another waiting ambulance where more paramedics took her vitals and strapped her in for a ride to the emergency room. *Lord, please let me go to the same hospital as Jake.* She needed to be able to pray as close to him as possible.

Dusk approached by the time the doctor was satisfied Beth's lungs had sustained no damage. She'd been placed on oxygen and assigned a bed in the emergency room. The doctor discharged her, leaving her to sit in the waiting area. She cradled a disposable cup of chilled water, reminding her of the glacier. If they'd survived that, they'd survive anything, right? Even a bullet. No one had been able—or perhaps willing—to give her an update on Jake. Her mind continued to go to the worst case. *He's not dead yet, they'd have told her.*

Special Agent Gregson's appearance as dark descended was the first sign of hope Beth had seen since Jake had been loaded into the ambulance. Surely the woman would give her some information.

"Miss Ryder, I'm glad to see you're in one piece. You've had quite a week." The agent's genuine smile thawed Beth's heart. This woman was hard to like, but maybe some humanity could be found in her heart after all.

"How's Jake? I mean, Deputy Cruz?"

Gregson frowned. "They didn't tell you?"

Beth's stomach lurched. "They've told me nothing. Is he okay?"

"He's in the ICU. Pulled through the operation, but he has a little way to go." Her voice was gentler than Beth expected. Had she given away her feelings? The agent continued. "He's in the best hands. The surgeon's top notch."

The platitudes reassured Beth a little, but not much. Jake

had *a little way to go*. Was that a euphemism for *Prepare for the worst*? She studied Gregson's face, but it remained neutral. Beth had to accept there was a chance Jake might not make it through the night. *Lord...please.* She didn't know what else to ask. Hopefully, He knew what weighed on her heart.

Gregson cleared her throat. "How about we go get some food? I don't know about you, but I haven't eaten in a while. Chang should be warming us a seat in the cafeteria."

Beth nodded and followed the agent to the cafeteria. "Don't I have another deputy assigned to me?" She swallowed, the uncertainty of the situation sending mild panic to her chest. Bakalov hadn't been arrested, as far as she knew. And Petrov hadn't been on the scene. He could still have someone find her in the hospital and take her out. If that happened, Jake's sacrifice would be in vain.

Gregson gestured for her to sit next to Special Agent Chang, who pushed a cup of tea and an unsavory-looking blueberry bagel with a pat of sad-looking butter in her direction.

The agent sipped her coffee before she spoke. "You did a great job, Miss Ryder. A really great job. So did Deputy Cruz. What you were up against..." Her voice trailed off and she shared a glance with Chang, who checked around the cafeteria. With evening visitors long gone, the space was mostly deserted. The few stragglers were outside hearing distance.

Gregson continued. "Mostly because of you, we've arrested the entire OCG, a large branch of the Russian mafia and Supervisory US Marshal Forsyth."

Beth's face fell. "What about Senator Bakalov? Surely you had enough to arrest him?" If not...the thought of reliving the past week, not to mention the last three years, filled her with a palpable dread.

"No." Chang leaned forward gave her hand a reassuring squeeze. Her heart gave a little pang as she thought about the far superior squeeze of Jake's hand. "Your testimony is no longer crucial. You can get your life back."

Beth's thoughts froze. What was Chang saying? *No longer crucial?* She ran her hands through her hair.

"I don't understand. I'm the only one who witnessed Petrov kill those men. If Jake isn't…? Who else can testify against Forsyth? And as for the Russians…" Her head spun.

"Bakalov." Gregson's words cut through her confusion.

"Bakalov? He and Forsyth were the ones striking the deal for me. They're old friends from school." Her heart lurched. "You're offering him a *deal*?"

Chang shook her head. "No." She shared another look with Gregson. Like they were silently debating whether to tell her something. "She deserves to know."

"Miss Ryder. Beth. You're very discreet, correct? Can we trust you to keep this information to yourself?" Gregson pursed her lips. It figured she'd be less trusting than Chang.

"I don't want you to get in trouble on my account." Beth frowned. As frustrating as this situation might be, Gregson and Chang had never given her a reason to distrust them. "If you promise you have this under control, I'll believe you. You don't have to tell me anything."

"Look, it's not exactly a state secret, but we'd appreciate you not telling anyone—except Deputy Cruz." Gregson took another sip of coffee and grimaced.

"Okay, now you've got me worried."

"Senator Bakalov works for us." Gregson dropped her voice. "He's been working undercover for us since before Petrov brought him into the gang."

Beth's eyes widened. "What?" The implications made heat rise up her neck. All this time, she'd thought she was alone. That *her* testimony was the only thing that guaranteed Petrov jail time. But someone else had been there the whole time! Not only that, but a man she'd believed was an enemy, not to mention a traitor. "Jake got shot for no good reason. I can't believe it!"

"Keep your voice down." Gregson reverted back to her usual, brusque self. "Deputy US Marshal Cruz did his job. He protected you." She gave Beth a pointed stare. "Please let me finish."

Beth clenched her jaw and wove her fingers together. Only fair to hear them out. Still, her mind returned to Jake's sacrifice. Would he be okay? No one had told her anything concrete about that, and Gregson's *a little way to go* didn't help. She tried to focus on the agent's words.

"You were exactly right about the senator, in a sense. You told us when we spoke last night that Senator Bakalov was probably beholden to the Russian mafia. That's correct. The Russians *had* bankrolled his family to an extent. He never personally took a dime, but he certainly benefitted from their money. The Russians believed that he would do whatever they wanted, and he let them believe that. When the time came for them to collect, though, he came to us."

Beth glowered. That figured. Who else could offer protection to a man who reneged on his promises to the Russian mafia?

"It's not what you think, Beth. We've interrogated him at length. The senator's an honest man. He's an American citizen, and a loyal one. He's genuinely grateful for all the opportunities this country has provided him and wanted to give back. But he couldn't do that if he was compromised. He also couldn't stand by and watch them get away with their criminal enterprises. The only way he saw through the dilemma was to work for the government.

"It's an incredibly brave thing he's done. Not only has he managed to take down Petrov's gang for good, he's rooted out a corrupt US marshal, and cut out the branch of the Russian mob that was flooding the northeast states with fentanyl. The senator has saved a lot of American lives, at great personal cost. He'll be under guard for the rest of his life." Gregson paused. "And he's got you off the hook. What you did helped Bakalov to bring to light a lot of criminal networks we couldn't touch. Without you, he couldn't have implicated the Russians this quickly. But you're small fry now. No one will much care about your evidence, and we won't even call you as a witness during the trials. We can use your affidavits if it comes to that."

"That makes sense, I guess…" Beth rubbed her hands on her legs, trying to release the frustration and tension that knotted in her shoulders. "But I don't understand Forsyth's role in this. How did he get involved?

Gregson leaned back. "That was unplanned. Forsyth asked Bakalov to help him get a significant promotion in return for handing you over to the OCG. Bakalov agreed, but Forsyth got greedy. When he realized the Russians were blackmailing Bakalov, he tried to get a piece of that action too. Didn't turn out well for him."

Beth shook her head in disgust. *O'Doherty paid for Forsyth's greed with his life.* One question remained. "Did you blow my cover?"

"What?" Gregson shook her head. "No. We'd never do that. Ever. We're assuming, until we find different, that it was that social media post you mentioned. But we're still looking, especially now we have Forsyth in custody. If there's another leak in the USMS, we'll find it."

Gregson's explanation made sense, but where did it leave her? The weight that should be lifting hadn't.

"What now?"

Gregson drained her coffee. "We'll have a formal debrief at our office tomorrow, then we'll take you back to Chicago, and you can go back to your old life. You're safe, Beth. Or should we call you Karina?"

The use of her birth name sounded foreign and familiar at the same time. Would she change it back? She'd grown used to "Beth." Despite her best efforts, she'd even made some good friends as Beth. Not to mention Jake. *Lord...please.* The words still wouldn't come.

"Beth is fine. Thanks."

My old life. Hadn't that been what she'd longed for these past three years? Hadn't she yearned to have her mom hold her? To go back to being an au pair? *No.* The word came before she could think any further. Sure, she'd see her mom the second she could, but her life wasn't in Chicago. It was in Cordova. *With Jake.* With Jake? Her eyes burned as she remembered the heaviness of Jake slumped on her, bleeding out. *He might die.*

The pain of that thought made it difficult to breathe. "Can you take me to Deputy Cruz, please? They might listen to you—your badge..."

Gregson and Chang stood, their faces grim. The women seemed to understand without any further words what Jake meant to her.

Ten minutes later, Gregson had negotiated half an hour of time for Beth beside Jake's bed. He lay unconscious, tubes poking through the bandages around his hands and from his nose and mouth. Even with the medical paraphernalia, his face seemed peaceful. At least compared to his usual look. A light stubble grew on his scalp and face. Like when they'd had to stay out overnight after their fall into the Matanuska River. Remembering that time sent a slight warmth through her chest. Jake had kept her safe then. He'd always kept her safe. Now he was paying the price. At least he hadn't been the first US marshal in history to lose his witness.

Swallowing back the tears, she reached for his hand and touched the fingers poking out of the bandage. "Jake, it's Beth. I don't know if you can hear me, but if you can…" What should she say? Something positive. "I know you're going to pull through." She grimaced. *Inspiring stuff.* Drawing a deep breath, she started again. "Jake, I'm sorry. I tried to escape, but I couldn't open the door…" He wouldn't mind about that, but she did. She'd tried so hard.

The memory of being trapped in the tool cabinet rose again, along with the calm that had enveloped her when she'd believed she was about to meet her Savior. Finally, words came to her.

"Lord, I know You were with me in the fire. I felt Your presence. You kept me safe. I'm trusting You to do the same for Jake now. Please protect him from death and heal his wounds. Amen."

Jake's eyelids were so heavy he couldn't open them. A series of annoying beeps prevented him from drifting back to sleep. Smells of bleach and ammonia assaulted his nostrils, and his parched mouth felt like it had been filled with cotton wool. Where was he?

"Jake?" The voice sounded familiar. "Are you awake? It's Beth."

Beth. He had to protect her. He forced his eyes open, and realized he was no longer on the floor of the hangar, but in a room full of hospital equipment.

A gasp, like a sob, came from his right, and Beth's face hovered above his. "Thank You."

Was she thanking *him*? Seemed unlikely. If he'd done his

job, she wouldn't have been in danger in the first place. His memory of what had happened remained fuzzy, but he knew it involved mistakes on his part. His eyelids failed him and he drifted back to sleep.

Next time he opened his eyes, Beth was gone. In her place, a nurse with slightly graying hair and a face mask held a folder in her hand and noted something down.

"Mr. Cruz, glad to see you're awake. My name is Sandy. I'm a nurse. You're in the intensive care unit, here in Anchorage. It's Thursday afternoon. You've been in and out of consciousness for almost two days. But I think you're going to be awake for a little longer this time because we've reduced your meds." Her voice was a little muffled by the mask, so she spoke loudly and slowly; he assumed to be heard better. "How's your pain?"

Jake couldn't feel a thing. "Fine." The croak that came from his mouth sounded like a common murre had taken up residence in his throat.

Sandy reached for a cup of ice chips. "Here, have one of these."

He sucked on the ice chip and tried to take in everything. Hadn't Beth been there earlier? "Beth?"

The nurse smiled. "Your friend? She'll be back soon." She returned the ice chips to the table. "Now, you're probably hungry, but we're keeping you on IV fluids for a little while longer. The bullet wound really did a number on your small intestine, so it needs a rest. The surgery went well, though, so you'll be back to solid food before you know it. The doctor will come to discuss the surgery and your treatment plan when he comes to check on you later."

A sharp intake of breath heralded Beth's arrival. "He's awake?"

"Yeah, I think you've got a good half hour or so before he

conks out again." Sandy smiled at Beth. "I'm done for now. I'll leave you to it."

"Thank you, Sandy." The relief on Beth's face almost broke Jake's heart.

Sandy gave Beth's shoulder a squeeze as she walked to the door and pulled the privacy curtain behind her.

Beth had begun to tear up, but she sniffed them back and straightened her shoulders. She opened and closed her mouth, then licked her lips. Maybe she didn't know what to say.

All the words he'd left unsaid swirled around his mind. They could wait. "It's good to see you."

Beth took a tentative step toward him, then another, until her leg brushed the edge of the bed. "I'm glad you're okay." She reached out her hand, then drew it back, uncertain.

Had she been holding his hand while he was out? He sure hoped so.

"I'm fine." A dull ache in his gut began, and he prayed it wouldn't get too much worse before Beth left. "Are you okay?" She looked wholly undamaged, if a little tired.

"Great, thanks to you." She smiled. "And the Lord."

The ache in his heart had nothing to do with his injuries. "You've been praying?"

"Nonstop." She sighed. "You gave me a real scare, you know?"

Thanks for answering our prayers, Lord. Now, please give me the words I need. He took a deep breath and did his best to reach out for Beth's hand, which had come to rest on the side of the bed. She reached to meet his fingers.

"You got some burns on your hands," she said, a nervousness entering her voice.

"They'll heal." He allowed himself to be drawn into her kingfisher-blue eyes and sent up one last prayer. "Beth, I love you."

Her eyes widened and her lips parted. "Love me?"

Doubt crept into Jake's heart, but he forced it away. If she didn't feel the same, he'd have to live with it. "Yes. I love you. I loved you when I kissed you, but I was too caught up in what that might mean for my job to put you first. I'm sorry for that, and I hope you'll forgive me."

A watery smile appeared, and Beth squeezed his hand. Yup, he felt those burns alright. But he didn't care. This was going in the right direction. Should he say more?

"There's nothing to forgive." She sniffed, swiping a tear from her cheek. "I was too scared of being rejected to believe you cared for me as anything more than a witness. But the truth is, I love you too."

She leaned forward and tentatively kissed him on the lips. Jake's heart raced, and warmth filled his body. She deepened the kiss, and an alarm went off.

Beth stepped back, her eyes fixed on the heart monitor. "Uh-oh."

Jake smiled. The kiss was worth it, and from the look on Beth's face, there'd be more where that came from. Many more. "You willing to take a chance on me?"

Beth nodded, her smile unwavering.

Sandy rushed back in, took one look at the two of them, then sighed, resetting the alarm. "Okay, lovebirds. I think it's time Jake had some rest."

"See you soon." Beth kissed him demurely on the cheek, then left.

Sandy checked his morphine and adjusted the dosage. "You've found a good one there."

"I know." Jake closed his eyes, feeling a deep contentment come over him.

Thank You, Lord, for all Your blessings.

EPILOGUE

One year later

Beth and Rachel walked through the door of Pamela's café to the smells of freshly-baked biscuits and coffee. A chill remained in the mid-May air, and a fire crackled invitingly in the hearth. Although grateful the journey had been via floatplane rather than ferry, Beth was still exhausted. Her hands felt empty without the armful of baked goods she'd usually bring to a social occasion. But she'd resolved to stop hiding behind the "baked goods lady" shield and let people into her heart.

"Pamela, we're here!" Beth called out. On Mondays, Café Valdez remained closed, so they were the only ones in the room.

"I'll be out in a sec, make yourselves comfortable!" Pamela's cheerful voice carried from the kitchen.

"Looks like this is for us." Rachel gestured to the table that had been laid for lunch with a white tablecloth, three lunch plates and sprigs of lilac- and lemon-colored primula in a small vase. "Aw, she's used the same napkins as your wedding!"

"Yeah." Beth smiled, running her hand over the simple,

silver-gray linen napkins Pamela had helped her pick six months ago.

Everything about her life had simplified since she'd accepted Jake's love. Their wedding had been a casual event, with their families and close friends congregating in Cordova, and Pamela overseeing the catering. Rachel's daughters Katie—well, Katie was technically Rachel's niece, but everyone thought of her as Rachel's daughter these days— and Sarah had been flower girls, with little Sarah toddling along nibbling rather than sprinkling the rose petals. Pamela and Rachel had been her bridesmaids, and her sister the matron of honor. Beth had let her hair fade to its natural color, allowed the curls to leave and worn her mom's white wedding dress.

Her wedding to Jake seemed like a long time ago, because so much had happened since then. True to their word, the FBI had released Beth from her obligations as a witness. With Senator Bakalov's help, the northeast branch of the Russian mafia had been dismantled, along with the remainder of Petrov's gang. Petrov himself had lost his appeal, and several further charges had been laid, ensuring he'd spend the rest of his life in prison. His children would never be subject to his harsh discipline again. Forsyth was also serving time in prison, having taken a plea deal. Senator Bakalov had just won a second term with a landslide victory.

Upon his release from hospital, Jake transferred from Chicago to the USMS Anchorage office. His hands had healed quickly and he'd returned to duty right after the rehabilitation. But he'd made a second change—having decided to transfer out of Witness Security and into Fugitive Investigations.

After their wedding, Jake had moved into Beth's house in Cordova. While he traveled a lot, Beth was used to keeping herself busy, and Jake made a point of keeping in touch. She smiled at the last message he'd sent before getting on the plane. Jake had finally tracked down and arrested a top Fifteen Most Wanted fugitive hiding out in Fairbanks. Ready to transport the prisoner to Anchorage, Jake had found time to take a selfie at the airport in seemingly broad daylight just before midnight. How the man seemed so chipper at that time of night always surprised Beth. The sun had set over Orca Inlet at around ten thirty, well past her bedtime, and she was deeply grateful for her blackout curtains!

"Welcome, ladies!" Pamela walked out from the kitchen, expertly balancing several plates of biscuits with jam and cream, along with tiny sandwiches and a plate of what looked suspiciously similar to Beth's signature coconut-mousse cookies. "Hope you're hungry!"

"I'm starving." Beth's stomach growled for emphasis, and Pamela and Rachel chuckled.

Setting down the plates of food, Pamela gestured for them to help themselves and returned to the kitchen, soon emerging with tea and coffee.

Once they were halfway through the feast, Beth jingled her knife against her teacup. "Now that my hunger pangs have gone, I have something to say."

Pamela wiped her lips with a napkin, and Rachel stopped chewing, mid-mouthful.

"Firstly, I want to thank you both for being such gracious, welcoming friends. I know I wasn't easy to get to know, but I appreciate your persistence. Having the two of you as friends means the world to me."

Rachel's eyes misted, and she swallowed her mouthful, reaching over to take Beth's hand to give it a wordless squeeze.

"Right back atcha, hon," Pamela said.

"Now before you say anything, there's more." Beth inhaled a deep breath and smiled.

Pamela raised an eyebrow.

"Jake and I will be parents in about six months' time. I'm pregnant!"

Squeals of joy filled the room, and Pamela and Rachel leaped to their feet, leaning in together to hug Beth.

"That's so exciting!" Rachel wiped a tear from her cheek. "You're going to be such an amazing mom."

"Congratulations, hon. Consider yourself in possession of a faithful babysitter." Pamela gave Beth a peck on her cheek.

As the women returned to their seats and resumed eating, arguing good-naturedly over whether the baby would be a girl or a boy, Beth's phone buzzed.

Jake: Have you told them?

Remembering the delight on his face when she'd confirmed he'd be a dad, she smiled, and texted back.

Yup, and I think we have our Godmothers lined up.

Love you so much.

The text came back immediately, and a warm glow settled in Beth's heart. The Lord was good.

* * * * *

Dear Reader,

Thank you for reading *Trapped on the Alaskan Glacier*. This is my second book set in the Cordova, Alaska, community, and I hope you've come to love the characters as much as I have. The moment I met Beth in *Alaskan Police Protector*, I knew she had some secrets. Uncovering them and giving her a deserving hero was so much fun. But Beth had some big challenges, especially when it came to opening herself up to others. Sometimes, it can be hard for us to trust others—even if we're not the heroine in a dramatic WITSEC storyline! Thankfully we have a completely trustworthy and faithful God, who loves us more than we can imagine. We can give Him our burdens, and—as Beth discovered—He is only ever a prayer away.

Blessings,
Megan

PS. I'd love you to sign up for my newsletter, please visit: www.meganshort.net.

Get up to 4 Free Books!

We'll send you 2 free books from each series you try
PLUS a free Mystery Gift.

FREE
Value Over
$25

Both the **Love Inspired®** and **Love Inspired® Suspense** series feature compelling
novels filled with inspirational romance, faith, forgiveness and hope.